KILLER KEYS

A COZY CORGI MYSTERY

MILDRED ABBOTT

WINGS OF INK PUBLICATIONS, LLC

KILLER KEYS

Mildred Abbott

for
Lois Smith
&
the Baldpate Inn

Cover, Logo, Chapter Heading Designer: A.J. Corza - SeeingStatic.com

Main Editor: Desi Chapman

2nd Editor: Ann Attwood

3rd Editor: Corrine Harris

Recipe and photo provided by: Baldpate Inn, Estes Park, Co. - The Baldpate Inn

Visit Mildred's Webpage: MildredAbbott.com

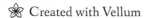 Created with Vellum

A knot began to form in my shoulders from gripping the steering wheel so tightly as I focused on Saint Vrain's twisting path, taking us ever higher into the mountains. Though it was only midafternoon, with the heavy clouds and the snowfall, the sun was little more than a hint of a glow behind the clouds that continued to grow heavier and heavier throughout the day. The town of Estes Park below us was nothing more than mist.

Even with the tension and concentration required for the treacherous roads, a sense of relaxed happiness washed over me. A weekend away! Though I was living my dream life, owning a perfect little bookshop in a gorgeously charming Colorado town, it had been forever since I'd had anything resembling a vacation. Maybe staying at an inn less than ten miles from my bookshop didn't technically qualify as a vacation, but I was going to count it nevertheless.

And I'd be surrounded by the people I loved the most. Life was good. So, so good.

The wintry scene of rugged peaks and jagged valleys filled with forests of pine and aspen covered in a thick blanket of snow was nothing short of spectacular. Despite the growing winter storm adding an ominous layer over the scene, I let out a long, contented sigh.

A pained grunt answered from the back seat of the Mini Cooper. I dared a glance from the winding, snow-covered mountain road to inspect the rearview mirror.

"Everything okay back there?"

Katie attempted a smile. "I'm regretting every single tr—" Her eyes went wide barely catching herself. "*T. R. E. A. T.* that I've made for our furry friend here. I never thought this sentence would leave my mouth, but I think it's diet time."

My overly *fluffy* corgi, Watson, paid the insult no mind and continued to shove his weight against Katie's lap in his attempt to wedge himself between the front seats of the car.

"I know you're excited to see me, little man, but we've got two whole nights together! There'll be plenty of bonding time." Beside me, Leo Lopez twisted around, simultaneously patting Watson and helping nudge his hearty backside off Katie's lap. "But if you crush our favorite baker, that's going to put a damper on the weekend."

Katie took a relieved breath, freed from Watson's... fluff... and swatted at Leo. "And if our favorite park ranger didn't have obnoxiously long legs, *he* could've squeezed himself in the back of the Mini Cooper and this whole situation would be avoided."

"Can't help how the good Lord made me." Stretching farther, Leo ruffled the fur between Watson's ears and then did the same to Katie's brown curls, earning himself another swat. "Plus, did I mention that I have claustrophobia issues?"

"Really?" Katie's tone held a glower. "Did I imagine sitting through a twenty-minute slideshow of your spelunking trip in New Zealand from a few years ago?"

Leo turned back around, chuckling. "That was different. I wasn't going to pass up my chance to see the *arachnocampa luminosa*."

Katie grunted again as Watson made yet another attempt to get to Leo. "Just because you know the fancy word for glowworm doesn't mean you're not riding in the back seat on the way home."

Overpowering a claustrophobic wave of my own at the idea of wedging through a tight dark cave miles below the surface of the earth, my contentment grew at my friends' bickering.

Leo had been gone during the first two weeks of January, visiting his family since he'd worked in the national park during Christmas. I'd missed him, maybe not with Watson's frantic enthusiasm, but... I cast another quick glance away from the road, taking in Leo's handsome features as he twisted back, making some comment to Katie once more. Before the holidays, I could've convinced myself I'd only missed him as a friend. Or at least enough that I would have been able to avoid looking much deeper. I couldn't do that anymore. And the awareness of his presence made my skin tingle to such a degree I marveled the two of them didn't pick up on it. Or knowing Katie and Leo, they probably did.

"Slow down." That time, it was Katie leaning up between the front seats, ducking her head so she could have a better view through the windshield. "I haven't driven up here very often, but I think this is one of my favorite formations in Estes Park."

Though I was already going slowly due to the

ice on the road, I eased off the gas a little more, and the three of us stared at the rocky cliffs surrounding the road, towering at least fifty feet above our heads. Directly in front of us, a tall, narrow opening cut through the rock like the eye of a needle, allowing us passage. It truly was breathtaking. "The last time I drove through it, I couldn't help but think that Watson and I were traveling into Narnia. I almost expected Aslan to be on the other side."

Katie snorted. "Instead you went to the home of the White Witch, and you weren't even turned to stone. It was a Christmas miracle."

"Oh, come on now." Though Leo clearly meant it as a reprimand, there was still humor in his tone. "Susan's not *that* bad."

"Surprisingly no, she isn't." I still couldn't believe the abrasive police officer lived in what almost equated to a storybook cottage. "However, ten to one, if she has trouble sleeping this weekend, she'll blame us for being so close to her house." As I spoke, we passed through the opening, and even though we hadn't actually entered a magical realm on the other side, the snowstorm did seem to increase instantly, the flurries making it harder to see through the windshield.

"They said it was going to be bad. Looks like they weren't wrong."

At the sound of concern in Leo's voice, I glanced his way. "Are you worried about the park?"

"No. Nadiya and the others have it under control, and it's not like there's anything I can do about the weather anyway. The animals take care of themselves." He studied the swirling mass of silver and gray in front of us. "Although, this is the longest I've been gone from the park since I moved to Estes. Feels a little strange. But when Percival and Gary asked me to attend, and it lined up so perfectly with the end of my trip, I wasn't about to say no."

And there was that tingling sensation over my skin once more. Every person taking part in the weekend anniversary celebration for my uncles was either family or longtime friends of Percival and Gary. Leo was the exception. They cared about him, but it wasn't like Gary and Percival ever hung out with Leo on their own. And he wasn't exactly considered family the way Katie was, either. He was something in the middle, something... different. The fact that my uncles had invited him to the anniversary party was a kind gesture, but it also lacked any subtlety, which was exactly what I would expect from Percival.

"There it is. On the left." Katie nudged my shoulder. "That's it, isn't it?"

Thankful for the distraction, I shoved thoughts of Leo and the obvious "setup" aside and followed where Katie pointed. "Good catch. I would've driven right past it." The carved wooden sign that read *Baldpate Inn* over the image of an old-fashioned key was nearly buried in the snow, as was the sharp turn from the highway into the trees.

"Good thing this baby does so good with winter weather." I patted the Mini Cooper's dashboard as I turned left. "But hold on, nevertheless."

Despite the snow tires, we fishtailed slightly over the ice as we rounded the corner and entered the lane cut between the tall trees.

Katie let out a little cry of surprise, and Watson took advantage of her distraction, gave a giant leap, and proved that despite his added padding, he could still claim moments of athleticism as he flung himself over the console between the front seats. His head banged my elbow, causing me to twist the wheel and send the car into a spin.

Gasping, I gripped tighter and used all my willpower to turn into the spin instead of the opposite way, as the trees blurred around us. After the first revolution, we'd slowed enough that I cranked the wheel slightly and hit the gas once more, and we shot off in our original direction.

Almost disbelieving, I glanced around, then sent Watson a glare. "If you kill your mama and her baker best friend, that's greatly going to impact the amount of treats you get."

Despite being wedged between the seats and grunting while Leo pulled him through and onto his lap, Watson issued a pleading whimper at the sound of his favorite word.

"Don't even think about it, buddy." I didn't bother looking at him, and only then realized my hands were trembling from the adrenaline.

Leo locked his arms around my corgi, not that he needed to bother. Now that Watson was on his lap, there was nowhere else he wanted to be. "That was impressive, Fred. If the whole bookselling and sleuthing thing doesn't work out, you can always be a racecar driver."

"No kidding." Though Katie sounded impressed, there was a waver in her voice that matched the shaking of my hands. "Don't take this the wrong way, but despite your skill, I think I'm never going to ride with you again. This is the second time we've almost died in one of your Mini Coopers."

Before I could comment on that, Baldpate Inn emerged, towering over us like a mirage in the snow.

"Wow!" Awe filled Leo's voice as he leaned over Watson to get a better view. "That is stunning."

"You've not been here before?"

He didn't look at me as he shook his head, completely focused on the old hotel. "No. I've heard about it, just haven't ever made my way up here."

"I haven't been here since I was a kid. We'd always come up here to eat when we'd visit my grandparents. It was one of my grandmother's favorite places." I slowed to a crawl, both because of the winter weather and simply to enjoy the sight.

"I've been reading about it," Katie piped up happily from the back.

Leo and I exchanged a quick, knowing glance. Katie was notorious for her Google binges.

"It's a century old and was named after a book. There's been a couple of plays and a movie based off it." Katie continued, either not noticing or not caring about Leo's smirk. "There's a tradition of hiring international students to staff the place, giving it a cosmopolitan kind of feel. And there's a collection of thousands and thousands of keys. In fact..." Katie's words trailed away to a wistful sigh as we drew nearer.

The century-old Baldpate Inn looked like a massive combination between a log cabin and a Swiss chalet. It had been built on the slope of the mountain, and nestled back into the trees. Its covered front porch jutted over the driveway, supported by massive logs. Smoke billowed from the chimneys, giving the large mansion structure a cozy, welcoming feel—a literal safe haven from the blizzard.

"Looks like we're the last ones here." I parked the Mini Cooper at the end of a long row of cars, each one belonging to a different member of my family.

"Sorry about that. I think after driving across the country the past couple days, my Jeep just decided it'd had enough."

"I didn't mean it like that. We're not late or anything. I'm glad you caught Katie and me before we left, so we were able to pick you up." Unbuckling my seat belt, I turned to Leo, hating the guilt I heard in his voice. "More, I meant it as a warning. We should all take a couple deep breaths now, because the minute we walk in there, we've got my whole crazy family to deal with. There's not going to be a moment's rest until the weekend is over."

He grinned, honey-brown eyes twinkling as he looked over at me, even as Watson lathered the underside of his jaw with kisses. "Knowing your uncles, it will be unforgettable."

"Don't let Percival hear you say that. Unforgettable doesn't cover it. Fabulous. He's been very adamant that the weekend is going to be *fabulous*," Katie piped up with a laugh, then shoved against the back of my seat. "Now, no more chitchat. Get out of this car. I feel like *I'm* the one who's been spelunking in New Zealand." She reached over and shoved Leo for good measure. "And if my leg cramps when I try to unfold from this pretzel shape I've had to be in, you're going to carry me, Smokey Bear. Put those muscles and long legs to some use."

Despite the building blizzard, I couldn't help but feel like I was slipping back nearly thirty years into my past as we made our way up the log staircase that opened to the expansive deck running along the front of Baldpate Inn. Though I barely spared a glance due to the cold, I could easily recall sitting at the edge of the railing with my grandmother, looking out over the panorama of mountains and the ant-sized version of Estes Park far below while scores of hummingbirds swarmed around us. Strange that I hadn't returned to the place since I moved. Even though the hummingbird feeders were empty and the birds themselves were surely tucked away in hibernation—or had flown south for the winter, I wasn't sure; I'd have to ask Leo—the place felt magical, just like when I'd been a child. No wonder

Percival and Gary had wanted to have their anniversary here.

Leo barely cracked open the front door of the inn before Watson darted inside as if he was on the verge of turning into an ice sculpture.

Katie followed him, chuckling. "The only one of us wearing an actual fur coat, and you'd think the poor thing was a hairless cat on an iceberg."

"Not to mention"—I smiled in thanks at Leo as I stepped past him into the warmth—"the added layers of insulation he's accumulated over the past year, *not* that I'm in any place to judge."

Leo closed the door, ushering in a last flurry of snow, and the three of us paused in the entryway. The magical feeling evaporated in the sense of tension that filled the space.

In front of us was an old-time check-in counter, complete with little cubicles on the back wall for each room. To the left, were the two rooms that made up the dining space, and on the right, seated in the overstuffed sofas arranged in front of the roaring river rock fireplace, was the source of the negative energy.

I nearly chuckled at the thought. *Negative energy.* Living close to my mother once more must've been having an effect.

My twin stepsisters, Verona and Zelda, book-ended their four children on the couches, their husbands, Jonah and Noah standing nearby, looking uncomfortable. Beyond them, standing in the doorway that led to two other rooms of the inn was my mother, stepfather, and Carl and Anna Hanson, who owned a high-end home furnishings store across from my bookshop.

The negative energy—I couldn't think of a more apt descriptor—radiated from my nieces and neph-ews. Ocean and Brittany, both fifteen, sat sullen-faced with their arms crossed. Leaf, who was nine, was red-faced, and from the streaks running down his cheeks, it appeared we'd just missed a break-down of epic proportions. Beside him, Christina, who was also nine, glanced up, and though she looked equally as devastated as Leaf, she cracked a small smile and twinkled her fingers toward Watson.

For his part, Watson didn't notice, instead giving a forlorn look up at Leo, as if apologizing for what he was about to do, and then issued a happy bark as he tore off across the space to collide into my stepfa-ther's shins.

Barry's laugh broke the tension, at least some-what, and he knelt to accept Watson's worshipful greeting. "Perfect timing, my furry little friend. We needed to be reminded of what matters."

Mom smiled at the sight of us and began to cross the room, but Leaf's wail cut her short. "Can't we just go home and get the—"

"If you ask that one more time, you won't see electronics again until you're in high school." Verona's bark caused me to flinch. She was slightly more serious than her sister, Zelda, but I'd never heard her snap like that toward any of the children. She careened around, offering a similar expression to her husband. "This is *your* fault, your obsession with electronics and gadgets and gizmos. I said I didn't want any of that stuff in my house, and now look at us. Five minutes being unplugged and it's a complete meltdown, making the entire family miserable."

Jonah blushed and stuffed his hands into his pockets, but didn't offer any more of a reply.

"Verona, let's just—" Zelda attempted a soothing tone, but didn't finish the thought when Verona's gaze flashed back her way.

The gorgeous room fell back into awkward silence, save for Watson's happy whimpering at Barry's ministrations.

Verona continued to glare at the children and finally looked toward Katie, Leo, and me. After a second, she sighed, and her shoulders slumped. "Hi, you guys. Sorry you had to walk in on this."

The rest of the room relaxed as one, sensing the worst had passed.

"It's okay. We all have our moments." I gave what I hoped was a carefree shrug. "Not even half an hour ago, Watson threw a fit when he was relegated to the back seat of the Mini Cooper, so we understand."

Verona attempted a tight smile, and I noticed Zelda wince.

Sometimes I forgot parents didn't appreciate a comparison between child-rearing and pet-ownership. Well... whatever. They were just jealous. A corgi never threw a fit that held an entire room hostage.

"In all fairness, I threw a similar one when *I* was *relegated* to the back seat as well," Katie chimed in, nonplussed. She shoved Leo, clearly trying to lighten the mood. "*This one* claimed it's because of his long legs, but I say it's pure and blatant misogyny."

Playing along, Leo raised his hand. "Guilty as charged."

Verona finally cracked a smile, but sent another glare toward Leaf. "One more word about any of it, and I promise you, *anything* requiring electricity gets donated or recycled the second we get home." She glared for a few seconds, then turned back to us. "We warned the kids that we wouldn't have any cell reception here, so we were prepared. However—"

"There's no Wi-Fi or computer access at all," Zelda jumped in. "*That* we weren't prepared for."

"Wait a minute..." All humor left Katie's tone. "You're telling me there's *no* internet? *At all?*"

Ocean, Leaf's older brother, smirked, clearly recognizing a kindred spirit.

I laid a hand on Katie's shoulder, lest whatever she said next caused my nephews and nieces to revolt. "I'm sure you'll survive two nights without Google."

She didn't reply, but her expression said she wasn't so certain of that.

"I am sorry." A voice pulled our attention back to the check-in counter, where a middle-aged woman with soft blonde hair emerged from the door behind the counter. "With it being slow season, it was the perfect time. We decided to have the inn rewired for high-speed internet, wireless"—she fluttered a hand —"the whole nine yards. With the building as old as this, we knew it wouldn't be a simple process, but it's been a nightmare. It was supposed to be done before Christmas, but..." She shrugged. "Here we are. I'm even having to run credit cards manually. Had to dig out that old swipey-machine thing." She walked around the counter and extended a hand, eyes twinkling. "I'm Lisa Bloomberg, owner of Baldpate, and destroyer of online entertainment, it seems."

I liked her instantly. "Well, I understand how that goes. Katie and I have closed the bookshop and bakery while we have an elevator installed to the second floor. There haven't been any huge glitches, but it's not exactly over yet." We'd given our employees a skiing trip during the time off as a late Christmas present.

"Speaking of which..." Katie gave me a meaningful look. "We need to call the contractor and give him the hotel's number in case there're problems, since our cell phones don't have reception here. I didn't even think before we left." She turned back to Lisa. "Do you have a landline phone?"

"We do." Lisa's eyes twinkled. "Not everything is a hundred years old here at Baldpate." She glanced at the few bags Katie, Leo, and I carried. "You have more luggage in your car? I can send Luca and Beau out to get it."

"Oh no. This is all we brought. But thank you." Leo glanced around, peering past the space into the room behind the glass French doors, the walls and beamed ceiling completely covered with keys. "I've never been here. This place is amazing."

"It is. Thank you." She grinned, pleased. "And I can say that with all humility since I'm not the one who built it, as I'm not a hundred years old either. I was actually getting ready to give a tour when..." She cast a hesitant glance toward the sofas, as if expecting another outburst. "Well, I can do that now as I show you three to your rooms."

"I would love that. I'm curious about the history of this place." Though Leo wasn't a native, his devotion to the national park had created a love of everything Estes Park.

"In a second." Mom finished her path across the room and pulled me down into a hug. "Good to see you, darling. It's beautifully bittersweet to be here again, isn't it?"

"It is. I think it'd make Grandma happy, everyone being together here again."

She patted my cheek before giving Katie and Leo welcoming embraces, as well.

The next minute or two was caught up in everyone greeting everyone. It was a beautiful aspect of living in a small town that I hadn't anticipated. We saw one another constantly, yet somehow, through all the events, celebrations, and bumping into one another, each and every time seemed special. Though sullen, even my nieces' and nephews' greetings were warm and sincere.

"We're missing some people. Where are the stars of the show?" I scanned the room again, realizing who else was missing besides my uncles. "And Gerald and Angus, they're supposed be here too, correct?"

Anna gave a long-suffering sigh. "Angus called Carl this morning. He and Gerald are driving up together, but of course..." She sighed again and judgment filled her voice. "They'll be running late because Gerald was finishing up his latest batch of kombucha. I swear that man ought to lose his license to practice law, considering—"

"Now, Anna," Carl broke in, "Gerald's a fine lawyer, and it's a free country. Just because..." His objection withered away under his wife's glare.

"And you know your uncles." Mom grabbed my hand as she lifted her voice, clearly jumping in before Anna could go on a tirade about all the reasons Gerald Jackson shouldn't be allowed to be a lawyer. And even though I was certain I'd agree with every item on the list, I was glad to avoid it. "They want to make an entrance." Mom chuckled. "Well... *Percival* anyway. They're staying in one of the separate cabins on the property—" She glanced toward Lisa.

"The Pinetop Sweetheart Cabin." Lisa waggled her eyebrows playfully. "It's like a little honeymoon suite, complete with a fireplace and a whirlpool."

"Oh..." Katie clucked, then continued in a swooning voice, "That's adorable, like a second honeymoon for Percival and Gary."

"Yes. Although, in this case, Percival is using it more as a cabin-sized closet. Never mind that we're only going to be here two nights. He brought enough clothes to have an outfit change every hour on the hour." Mom shook her head, grinning. "Which is exactly why they're not here yet. I'm sure Percival is primping for his grand arrival. Gary's probably watching football."

"No..." Lisa sounded hesitant. "The televisions are out of service as well."

One of the kids groaned in forlorn despondency, followed by Verona issuing a swift shushing sound.

"Don't you worry about it for a second." Mom patted Lisa's arm. "I think it worked out wonderfully. Three days and two nights of nothing but family time and bonding. It's perfect."

"And if anyone gets bored, we have plenty to entertain us." Barry gave me a quick hug as Watson pranced happily back and forth between him and Leo. "Not to mention more wonderful food than we can possibly eat. Not that we aren't already used to that." He gave Katie a hug as well before offering one to Leo.

Within another five minutes, Lisa led Katie, Leo, and me on the tour. Mom, Barry, Anna, and Carl joined in. Zelda, Verona, and their families retired to their rooms, deciding to regroup before Percival and Gary made their entrance. Lisa directed us to a staircase that ran up along the far wall of the main room, and we headed upstairs, the old wooden steps creaking comfortingly under our weight. "Let's drop off your bags first." She motioned down the hallway to her left, and we all followed. She gestured toward a small room. "Mr. Lopez, this is you."

"We're right across the hall, dear." Mom tapped the old-fashioned doorknob of hers and Barry's room.

Barry chuckled. "Yes, in case you get scared in the middle of the night and have a bad dream, you can have Mom and Dad soothe you back to sleep."

Mom swatted at him. "You know what I mean. I know Leo's not a child."

Though Leo grinned, his gaze flicked to me, just for a second, and my heart... well... I didn't give my heart long enough to decide what it did exactly.

Lisa didn't pause as Leo dropped off his bag, and she headed to the end of the hallway to unlock the last door on the right. "Ms. Page, Ms. Pizzolato, this is your room."

"And we're right across the hall from you." Anna sounded excited, as if she was envisioning late-night gossip sessions.

As we entered the room, Katie and I both paused. It hadn't been updated. It wasn't sleek-or-shiny modern. The walls were log, the floor was old planks, the ceiling exposed log beams. Between the two beds in the center of the long narrow room was an old porcelain sink.

"Oh, I love it." Katie sighed. "It's like we're staying in a Colorado version of *Little House on the Prairie*."

Lisa laughed, almost sounding relieved. "That's a new description; I like it. I'm glad you're pleased. Sometimes people are irritated when the rooms don't look like they just stepped into the Ritz."

Barry scoffed. "That would ruin the whole thing."

"I quite agree." Taking a cue from Watson, though I didn't follow his example of sniffing around the floor as he wandered around, I walked through the room, pausing by the bed to touch the beautiful patchwork quilts, tracing my finger over the golden key stitched in the center. "This is wonderful."

"Thank you. I made one for each bed in the inn." Pride filled Lisa's voice. "Keys are very important. Baldpate was inspired by the 1913 novel *Seven—*"

"*Seven Keys to Baldpate.*" Katie, true to form, sounded like the girl in class jumping up and down in her seat while she raised her hand and answered the question before the teacher could even finish. "Seven strangers were given the keys to an old mountain hotel. It didn't end well for them. It's also been made into a couple of plays and a movie from the 1940s."

Lisa looked impressed. "You've read it?"

Katie flushed and I answered for her. "No, but Katie is a master of trivia." I slid my bag off my shoulder and placed it on the bed. "I started reading when Percival and Gary decided to have their anniversary here. It's kind of like an old-fashioned cozy murder mystery, though I must confess I have to keep reminding myself not to judge how women are described since the book was written over a hundred years ago."

"Yes, times change, thankfully." Lisa smiled again. "But I find it a lovely part of our history."

At that moment, the windows rattled, and the

wind howled. Watson whimpered and scurried over to take his place beside me, a low growl emanating from his chest.

I moved across the room, Watson at my heels, and peered out. Though it was still before sunset, it was nearly dark outside, the scene little more than a grayish-white blur through the windows.

"Typically you'd have one of the best views from this room." Lisa moved beside me and peered out. "The way it sounds, you won't have much of a better view tomorrow. Maybe on the day you leave."

With our bags deposited, Lisa continued the tour, Leo joining us as we passed back in front of his room. She gestured down the hall that ran behind the stairs. "That's the staff wing. You may know this, but Baldpate prides itself on hosting international students, some of them here for college, others simply here to have an American experience for a year or so. Right now we have young adults from Germany, France, Holland, Italy, and England." She snickered. "And one from Arkansas, of all places. They're good kids, and I promise you they won't be loud or disruptive during the night. Most of them are taking a break right now before the party this evening, and the rest are cooking away."

The inn was shaped like a broken cross—a long

center hallway and then two jutting off on either side, one sitting a little farther back than the other. When we passed the steps, Lisa pointed. "The east wing has our other guest rooms. That's where the twins and their families are staying as well as Mr. Witt and Mr. Jackson when they arrive."

Once back downstairs, Lisa led us through the larger dining room. Baldpate was unique in that it didn't offer a menu of normal food items. It was simply an all-you-can-eat salad bar that was situated in an old cast-iron bathtub. It also hosted several varieties of homemade bread, an assortment of stews and soups, and made-from-scratch pies placed near an old iron stove in the middle of the room. I could practically feel Katie's sensation that she'd died and gone to heaven. The second dining space was adjacent to the first but attached through two sets of French doors. The closed-in porch was filled with rustic log tables, and the wall of windows that curved around the space showed just how ominous the storm was becoming.

"Once more, typically you can see Estes Park snuggled into the valley, the whole mountain range, and beyond." Lisa leaned in close to one of the windows. "I can't even see the trees on the other side of the driveway. It's been years since we've had a storm this bad."

Leo moved beside her, concern etching his face. "It seems like they were off on their predictions. It's a lot worse than what they told us. Doesn't look like it's even considering slowing down."

"Are you worried? Do you feel like you need to leave?" Without thinking, I stepped to him and put my hand on the back of his shoulder.

Leo flinched slightly and glanced toward his shoulder, then at me. Some expression I couldn't read crossed behind his eyes, but whatever it was lightened the concern that had been there. "No. There's nothing I can do. It simply is what it is. I just hope no one is foolish enough to go out in it."

I dropped my hand, wondering if anyone else had noticed the gesture.

Lisa continued the tour before I could check. "Now, if you'll follow me, I'll show you the key room. It's my favorite place in Baldpate." She led us back past the check-in counter and paused by the roaring fireplace. "Remind me to show you this later. Right now I don't want to interrupt the dinner preparations, but the fireplace is double-sided. If you pass through the door, you'll enter the staff lounge surrounded by the kitchen. But the key room is where—"

At that moment, the front door of the lodge burst open, followed by a whirlwind of snow.

Watson yelped, dashed underneath my skirt, and then poked his head out to begin barking.

Leo chuckled affectionately. "So brave."

"We're heeeerrrreeee!" Percival emerged through the blizzard, long, lanky arms lifted above his head as if he were Marilyn Monroe arriving at a star-studded gala. He did a little twirl, which fanned out the nearly floor-length tails of his white, rhine-stone-encrusted tux jacket. The rest of his outfit, from the shoes, to the slacks, to the shirt, tie, and vest, to his top hat, were a deep wine-red purple. "Let the festivities begin!"

Percival's eyes narrowed as he glanced around the main room and peered behind him into the dining spaces, before looking back at us in accusation. "Where is everyone?" He did a quick finger-count. "Over half the group is missing."

Gary shut the door behind them, cutting off the billows of snow, then dusted the piles of flakes from the shoulders of his tux. He'd gone classic elegance and looked more handsome than I'd ever seen him. "I told you we should've called over and said we were arriving if you really wanted to make an entrance."

Percival considered and then scowled. "Well, it is what it is. I'm not going out there just to come back in. The snow is ruining my suede shoes."

"I told you suede wasn't a good—" Gary shut his mouth with Percival's second glare, then caught my bemused look from across the room and winked.

I adored the two of them. So different and yet perfectly matched.

Before anyone could respond, there was a clatter down the steps and my four nephews and nieces arrived, followed by Verona, Zelda, Noah, and Jonah. Thankfully, the tension they'd carried with them earlier seemed to have dissipated. Zelda halted at the base of the steps when she caught sight of Percival and Gary. "You're here! Look at you, aren't you both smashing!"

"I believe the word is *fabulous*," Leo blurted out, then went scarlet.

"Exactly so! And yes, we do, yes. Thanks for noticing." Percival barked out a laugh, and pointed at Leo before narrowing his eyes at the twins. "Even if you did spoil the entrance." When Gary shoved his shoulder, Percival smiled. "But... not a big deal. I plan on making more than *one* entrance this weekend." He stepped forward, opening both arms wide. "Thank you all for being here. It means the world to us to be surrounded by those we love. Now... lavish us with your affections."

The next several minutes were lost to another round of greetings, hugs, and congratulating Gary and Percival on their anniversary. The cold outside was forgotten, as well as the drama over no connection to the outside world as we fell into step being together.

Lisa cleared her throat to get our attention. "Dinner is on schedule, but we can wait for the others if you want. That's a good thing about a salad bar, it's flexible, and the soups and stews aren't going to be spoiled by simmering. We can get to the key room later."

Barry, who was kneeling by Watson, spoke up decisively. "I say we go ahead. We love Gerald, but even without a blizzard the man would be late to his own funeral."

"Doubly true since he's messing around with his demon liquor," Anna mumbled under her breath, but nudged Leo with her elbow. "You're law enforcement. Can't you do something about that?"

"Anna!" Carl hissed. "Stop that. It's not illegal, and it's not liquor."

Leo simply chuckled. "And I'm not exactly law enforcement. Unless Gerald is somehow using his homemade kombucha to poach protected species of wildlife, I think he's a little bit out of my jurisdiction."

Anna looked unsatisfied with that answer, but then her eyes brightened, and she smacked Carl's arm. "Oh, I just remembered. We left the treats we brought for Watson in the car. Go get them."

Carl gaped at the door, then back at her. "Right now? We're just getting ready to sit down to dinner, and there's a blizzard."

"Well, then I guess you should have remembered to bring them in the first place, shouldn't you? Surely you don't expect sweet little Watson to sit there in forlorn depression while we have dinner and he has nothing special?"

"Anna, it's okay. Trust me, Watson's not going to starve. There'll be some things he can—"

She cut me off with another swat at her husband. "The quicker you go, the quicker you'll return."

"Fine. Let me go get my jacket," Carl grumbled as he turned and trudged back up the steps.

I studied Anna for a second. She was always rather bossy with Carl, but it seemed a little mean, even for her.

As if feeling my gaze, Anna clapped her hands and lifted her voice. "I agree with Barry. Let's eat!"

Lisa waved us forward. "All right then, follow me." She led us from the place in front of the fire to the buffet spread out over ice in the clawfoot bathtub. "We have the salad bar with all the fixings, of course, and down here we've got our world-famous cornbread, loaves of honey-wheat bread, apple-raisin spice muffins, green-onion cream cheese muffins, and our Swiss knots." She walked toward the center of the room where three black kettle warmers were arranged on a separate table. "Tonight we have the Baldpate cowboy buffalo stew, red chili, and a broccoli cheese soup." Finally Lisa moved to another table filled with pies. "For dessert, there's a selection of Keyroom lime, coconut angel cream, chocolate cream, Baldpate rhubarb, Key pecan, and Scandinavian apple."

Beside me, Katie whimpered, then turned her wide brown eyes up at me. "How have you never brought me here?"

"I was wondering the same thing myself." I patted my stomach, the memory of the cornbread drifting back from childhood. "I think the next time we take a weekend away from the bookshop we might need to attend one of those diet camps."

A look of genuine utter horror flitted over Katie's face. "I think that's the ugliest thing I've ever heard you say."

Laughing, I threw an arm over her shoulder and gave her a squeeze. "And this is why we work, you and me."

Before long, we were all spread out over the

small log tables that filled the glassed-in porch. The dining room was beautiful, but there was something lovely about being clustered together with the blizzard blowing outside as we lost ourselves to the warmth and comfort of delicious soups and stews and the yeasty perfection of the assortment of breads. At times when the blizzard softened just a bit, the twinkling lights of Estes Park could be seen far below.

Watson was in corgi heaven as he wandered from table to table and followed people around while they made trips back and forth from the buffet line, scooping up any scraps that fell quicker than any Hoover could boast.

Anna returned from her second trip to the salad bar, her plate laden with cornbread and muffins, and paused before she took her seat at the table behind Katie, Leo, and me. "I just realized, Carl still hasn't returned." She stepped closer to the window, pressing her hand against the glass and trying to peer down. "Maybe I shouldn't have sent him outside."

"Is he a heavy man, miss?" Our adorably young German waiter appeared from nowhere. "Glasses, and with a fuzzy beard?"

Anna turned slowly from the window, her hand

lowering from the glass to rest on her girth. "He's *big-boned*, yes."

The waiter nodded enthusiastically, pointing out the window where Anna had been looking. "I noticed him in the parking lot a few minutes ago with two other men."

"Two other—" Her voice lowered. "Oh really. Were they drinking something?"

He nodded again. "Yes, ma'am."

She growled. "I'm going to murder him." Then she piped up, "What was your name, young man?"

"Luca, ma'am."

She patted his hand. "Well, Luca, keep an eye on that one for me and report back, and I'll make sure you get a special tip at the end of the weekend."

Impossibly, Luca brightened even further. "Yes, ma'am!"

Katie leaned into the table so only Leo and I could hear her. "What's up with Anna and her tirade against the kombucha?"

"Don't you remember? Gerald makes his kombucha with cannabis-infused tea." I cast my glance over to where Mom and Barry were seated with my uncles. Mom was aware that Barry liked to partake in edibles from time to time, but I didn't want to bring up any sore subjects.

"From the looks of things, it appears Gerald might be starting a war with Anna." Leo chuckled. "Good luck with that, buddy."

As if on cue, the front door burst open as Carl and Gerald tumbled in laughing and accompanied by a fresh gust of wind and snow. The more subdued owner of the knitting store downtown, Angus Witt, followed behind them, shutting the door once more.

Carl's laughter faded as he noticed Anna standing between the tables, hands on her hips. He cleared his throat and then lifted a cardboard box. "I was... helping them bring in their luggage."

"Sure you were." Anna folded her arms. "Did you even remember Watson's treats?"

Watson scurried over at the word, and Carl's face fell even further.

"That's okay! Believe me, Watson's fine. We all are." I jumped up before Anna could tell him to go back out into the snow. "Why don't the three of you grab some food and join the celebration?"

Anna looked like she was about to argue, but Percival intervened. "And hurry it up, you three. It's about time for speeches, and I don't want any of you to be deprived of telling me how wonderful I am." Mom swatted at her brother, and he sighed good-naturedly before kissing Gary on the cheek. "How wonderful *we* are, I mean, of course."

"In high school, I was desperately in love with the star quarterback." Percival stood at the table, a glass of champagne in one hand, his other on Gary's shoulder, and the blizzard raging behind his back. "Of course, he didn't know I was alive. Which is a good thing as he would've beat me to a pulp."

He laughed, and most of the room chuckled with him. I did as well, though I couldn't help but marvel at the strength and bravery my flamboyant, and often flighty, uncle possessed. I could only imagine what it would have been like going through high school in a small town as a gay kid over sixty years before.

"I never would've guessed I'd end up spending my life with an ex-pro-football player." Percival ran his hand over Gary's broad shoulders in a rare tender gesture, then he bugged his eyes and returned to his typical showmanship. "Somebody should've warned me how many hours I'd be forced to watch sports on television! Let this be a lesson, kids." He held his champagne flute aloft, and everyone clinked their glasses together.

"Ever the romantic." Gary stood, his low rumble

of a voice barely audible over the howls of the wind outside. "My dad wanted me to marry one of the cheerleaders." He winked at Percival. "I came pretty close."

Percival shimmied his narrow shoulders, causing the light to glisten off the rhinestone-encrusted jacket, sending rainbows around the room. "I have no idea what you mean."

Gary laughed, and the adoration he felt for his husband, even after their decades together, was on full display. Then he turned toward the rest of us, growing slightly serious, his dark eyes flitting over the tables and then pausing at me. "I think the real lesson is to find someone who causes you to laugh, helps you feel safe, and makes breathing just a little bit easier." Then his gaze moved on, and his tone brightened as he launched into the story of when he and Percival first met.

I only half listened, trying to get my racing heart under control, making sure that no emotion or nerves played over my face. I dropped my hand beside my chair, and sure enough, my fingertips found Watson's pointy fox ears waiting, and I stroked his head. He always knew when I needed him. And like every time before, just his presence soothed.

I'd spent the past weeks since Christmas not thinking. I'd used a lot of energy to *not* think.

There'd been a moment between Leo and me late afternoon Christmas Day when my family had gone sledding at Hidden Valley. I thought he'd been about to kiss me, and if I'd been reading him correctly, I think he thought the same thing. But that wasn't the moment. Well... it was, but the perceived near-kiss was merely the catalyst. Something clicked in that moment. It had flitted around me since I'd met Leo. I'd kept it at bay—at times it was little more than an awareness, and at others I'd had to beat it back with a baseball bat.

There'd been a million reasons. I hadn't moved to Estes Park for a relationship, hadn't even wanted one. There was a life to reinvent, a bookstore to open, family to reconnect with, unexpected murders to solve. Leo was eight years younger than me, and prettier than I was. Both thoughts shallow and ultimately unimportant... but they'd been there. And then there'd been... *whatever* it had been with Sergeant Branson Wexler. Not quite a romance, but... kind of.

In that moment at the base of the sledding hills of Hidden Valley, after all the reasons to ignore or pretend it was something other than it was, my guard slipped, and some puzzle piece clicked into place. It snapped so loudly that I couldn't pretend I didn't feel it, and from the expression that crossed Leo's face, I could've sworn he heard it too.

But then Leaf's sled crashed into Christina's, and there was much screaming and laughing. The moment passed, and we didn't mention it again.

After, Leo left to visit his family, and I threw myself into the bookshop, bringing in the New Year and helping Katie get the bakery ready to be shut down while the elevator was installed. I hadn't allowed myself to think of it, not the worries or the hopes. To the point that Katie was frequently asking me what was the matter. That I seemed distant, shut off. She hadn't been wrong. I'd felt a million miles away, even to myself.

But there, in the middle of family and friends, the snowstorm circling the inn, my uncles celebrating their love and the life they'd built together, with Watson's comforting presence at my fingertips, something cracked, and it all began to seep back in.

My heart thundering, I angled my head just slightly so I could study Leo's profile as he focused on Gary's speech.

Leo was handsome, breathtakingly so, but that didn't have anything to do with it, at least not much.

There'd been so much uncertainty, so much loss

in my life, not just in the past year, though that had been enough. Being involved in solving murders and then being betrayed by a man I thought I could trust. But, before that, there'd been my ex-husband's affair, our divorce, the duplicity of my best friend and business partner as I was cut out from our publishing house.

My father's murder.

From the second I'd met Leo Lopez, even with my nerves and the ridiculous number of butterflies in my stomach that left me tongue-tied, I felt safe with him. And while Leo didn't make me laugh like he was some great comedian, he made the moments he was near brighter. And he definitely helped me breathe easier.

It happened again, as I studied him. That click. Well... that's not exactly right. It hadn't ever unclicked. I was simply forced to admit it again. Leo and I hadn't dated. Hadn't kissed. Nothing like that. We were friends, best friends. He, Katie, and I were the Three Amigos. It was one of the ways I'd been able to shove it aside. But even without any of the romantic buildup, dating—whatever the steps were supposed to be—I knew. Maybe he had known the whole time.

Probably feeling me studying him, Leo turned

slightly, his honey-brown eyes catching my gaze, and he started to smile, then flinched ever so slightly, and his eyes widened.

He could see it. Even though I attempted to throw the walls back up, Leo could see it. The corners of his lips finished their curve into a smile, one more self-conscious than I was used to seeing from him, and I could feel the hum of energy build between us.

We both jumped when the front door of the inn burst open behind us, and for what felt like the millionth time that night, a torrent of wind and snow gushed in.

As one, everyone in the anniversary party turned and looked toward the door. A group of women, each loaded down with a suitcase or two, bumbled inside. It was like they wouldn't stop coming. Three, then four. By the time the sixth one entered, the first few had started taking off hats and scarves.

The one in front ran fingers through smashed stylish blonde hair, and her eyes widened when she saw all of us staring at them. "Sorry to interrupt! We're a little early."

An African-American woman beside her chuckled. "I think an entire day is a bit more than a *little* early."

As the squeak of the door opening and closing sounded, Lisa Bloomberg hurried out from behind the check-in counter. "We're in the middle of a private party, I'm sorry. May I help you?"

The blonde spoke again. "Yes. We're not supposed to check in until tomorrow. The plan was to spend the night in Denver, but the storm was getting so bad we decided to forge ahead. We tried to call, but it didn't ring through."

Confusion flitted over Lisa's face, then seemed to clear. "Oh. You're the um... knitting group?"

Before they could answer, a seventh woman entered, slamming the door shut behind her before ripping off her hood. She was gorgeous and a couple decades younger, from what I could tell of the group. She tossed a snow-covered bag on the floor. "You really need to get someone out there to clear your driveway. The snow was over my knees. Our vans practically slid all the way down the drive. You're just begging for a lawsuit."

At Katie's intake of breath, I glanced her way. Her brows knitted and an atypical hostile expression flitted over her face as she looked at me. "Alexandria Bell. I can't stand that woman."

FOUR

After welcoming the women to take off their coats and warm up in front of the roaring fire, Lisa hurried through our party and headed directly to Percival and Gary. They were seated close enough she was easily overheard. "I'm so, so sorry. I know you wanted the inn all to yourselves this evening. This was the group that I told you would show up tomorrow night."

"Don't you stress. It's not a big deal." Gary didn't miss a beat before he reassured her. "There's enough room, more than enough food, and it's not like we don't see one another all the time. The more the merrier."

Relief flooded her features. "Are you sure you don't mind?" She glanced toward the larger dining room. "I imagine it will take us a little while to get settled. I can serve them dinner in about an hour, try to give your group time to wind down, or—"

"Whenever is totally fine. Including right now. Sounds like they've had a rough go of it." Gary cut her off with a friendly pat on the back. "No need to make them wait."

Percival, however, had narrowed his eyes and weaved his head as he tried get a better view of the group of women, then turned and looked at Angus, his eyes twinkling. "Your gal pal is early!"

"She's..." Angus's cheeks pinked, and he gave an exasperated huff. "I'm sorry." Without another word, he headed toward the group of women.

"Angus has a gal pal?" Beside me, Katie stood on tiptoe and leaned to get a better view around Leo's shoulder.

Leo chuckled. "People still use the term *gal pal*?"

"Oh, hush up." Katie angled farther around him. "That's adorable. I wonder who..." Her words faded away as a horrified expression washed over her face.

Angus beelined directly toward Alexandria, took her by the elbow, and led her toward the far corner.

"Well, that's just disgusting." Katie sounded revolted.

"Oh, come on now." Leo nudged her with his

elbow. "So she's a little younger than Angus. It's not a big deal." He shot me a glance but looked away quickly, as if he knew the eight years between us gave me pause.

"A *little*? Try three decades." Katie elbowed him back. "But that's not the issue. Angus is a total sweetheart. Alexandria... isn't."

"You can say that again." Anna arrived at our table, causing Watson to look up in excited anticipation, equating her arrival with his favorite treats. For the second time that night, she let him down, and on this occasion didn't even notice him. "She's nothing but a highfalutin man-eater. I don't know what Angus sees in her." She sniffed. "Well... yes, I do. Just goes to show, even men who are as kind and classy as Angus Witt are still just *men*."

From what I could see, it *was* an odd pairing, but I took Anna's claim with a grain of salt. Alexandria wouldn't be the first woman Anna had labeled a man-eater. I put more stock in Katie's reaction; she got along with everyone.

The anniversary party settled back down, though Angus didn't return. As Lisa and the rest of the staff got accommodations sorted for the group of women, we refocused on Gary and Percival, listening as they shared memories of their life together and offering a few of our own.

By the time we'd started the dessert round, and our tables were laden with pies, the staff had refreshed the salad bar, breads, and soups, and the newly arrived group was gathered around the large circular table in the other room.

I was halfway through my piece of rhubarb pie when I realized Watson was no longer between Leo and me. I did a cursory glance toward Barry, certain that I'd see him. But he wasn't there. I started to rise, just a touch of panic flickering in me. It wasn't like Watson to wander away, but there'd been a lot of going in and out of the front door as the rest of the group's luggage had been brought in. There was a chance he'd darted outside and gotten trapped.

"Watson's over there." Leo's whisper was gentle, and he gestured with his head toward the other room. "He's making friends."

Of course Leo knew where Watson was. I looked to where he'd indicated, and found Watson plopped beside the chair of one of the women. Strange. Making friends wasn't one of Watson's typical activities. Then I did the math, which should have been obvious enough. Making friends might not be a motivator, but begging for food most definitely was.

I finished standing and excused myself. "I'll be right back."

I slowed as I approached the table. Unless I was reading the situation wrong, Watson wasn't begging. Instead he was sitting contentedly beside one of the older women as she scratched behind his ears and cooed sweetly to him.

There didn't appear to be any food motivation at all.

Maybe the snowstorm had thrown him off.

"I'm so sorry. I didn't realize my dog had wandered off." All six women looked up at me as I approached. There was an empty chair, which I assumed was for Alexandria. She and Angus still hadn't returned. "Watson will eat you out of house and home if you let him."

"Watson." The one who'd been petting him smiled down at him affectionately. "That suits you. You look like a Watson."

In response he shoved his nose against her palm, demanding more affection. She obliged, lowering her other hand to scratch Watson's side.

What in the world? "He really likes you."

Watson shot me a glance that clearly said, *Don't you dare ruin this for me, lady.*

"You must be a corgi whisperer." I knelt beside him so I was on level with the seated woman. "Watson hardly likes anybody."

Still petting him, she shrugged, lifted her blue eyes to mine, and smiled. "No, I'm just good with animals. I grew up on a farm." She chuckled. "Still live on that farm, so there's been a lot of animals through the years. And we always have at least one dog running around."

She could shrug it off all she wanted; there was one thing I'd learned—when Watson responded so powerfully to a person, they were someone to be trusted. The opposite wasn't always true, as he truly wasn't a people person. There were plenty of perfectly wonderful people who Watson wouldn't give the time of day, but he most definitely didn't fawn over someone who wasn't exceptional. Leo and my stepfather were proof of that. "Well, I appreciate you letting him interrupt your meal." I offered my hand. "I'm Winifred Page, Watson's mama. But everyone calls me Fred."

Sure enough, the second she removed one of her hands from Watson to take mine, he shot me another glare.

"Nice to meet you, Fred. I'm—"

A sharp intake of breath cut her off, and I looked up to see the blonde with the perfectly coiffed hair I'd noticed earlier, gaping at me. "Winifred Page... and a corgi." Her blue eyes, which matched the other woman's, looked from me, down to Watson, then back up. "*You* own the Cozy Corgi Bookshop."

I was a little taken aback. "Yes. I do."

The woman's tone grew more excited. "Then you know Katie Pizzolato!"

"I... do." Caution bells went off in the back of my mind. If this was someone from Katie's past, she might not have the best of intentions. It wouldn't be the first time Katie's history had come calling. From the lady's tone, she sounded like Santa Claus had just come down the chimney as opposed to plotting some murderous revenge. "Do... *you* know Katie?"

"Oh no! But I'm dying to." The blonde went into cheerleader hyperdrive. "She's the reason we're here. Well... kind of. I found out Alexandria was coming to Estes Park. And of course, we all know about Knit Witt's—we're a knitting club, you see. So we're dying to see his store—but really, it's Katie I wanted to meet. I've been dying to for months."

Again I didn't hear any hint of malevolence in her tone, more like a rabid boy band fan than anything, but it didn't make sense. I knew Katie was the object of many speculative conspiracy theories because of her parents' criminal pasts, but this lady didn't look like the type to be intrigued by that. Still, you never could tell. "Why do you want to meet Katie?"

"Oh my goodness, I got carried away. I'm sorry. You must think I'm insane." The woman fluttered her hands excitedly. "I'm a devout follower of *The Sybarite*, and ever since a review of the bakery came out, I've just been desperate to visit. This perfectly cozy little bakery on top of a perfectly cozy little bookshop nestled in a perfectly cozy little mountain town? Well... it just sounds... perfect."

"And cozy, apparently." The older woman with the matching blue eyes and the object of Watson's crush laughed indulgently.

I relaxed instantly. Our friend Athena Rose was the author of that particular food blog, though she wrote it under the pen name Maxine Maxwell. So the woman's adoration was based around pastries, not murder. That was a good sign.

The blonde continued, undeterred. "If the snow thins out tomorrow, I hope we can go down into town and visit the bakery. I plan on sampling every single thing there."

"Oh, I'm sorry." I patted Watson's head and stood, my knees refusing to remain in the hovering position any longer. "We're doing some renovations in the bookshop and bakery. It's closed for the next several days." The woman's face fell, and I hurried on. "But you can still meet Katie. We're up here for my uncles' anniversary, and Katie's with me. I know that doesn't help with sampling the baked items, but—"

"Oh no, that's wonderful! Thank you!" The woman clapped, pleased once more, and stuck out her hand. "I'm Pamela." She gestured toward the other woman. "This is my sister, Cordelia."

Once more, Cordelia lifted a hand from Watson and shook mine. "Pleasure to meet you. And I'm so sorry we interrupted your party." Before I could respond, she pointed around the table, each of the women nodding in turn. Most of the women appeared to be in their fifties and sixties, with a couple of notable exceptions. "The rest of our little knitting entourage are Wanda"— she indicated to the African-American woman I had noticed when they came in. "Betsy, Minnie, and Cassidy." Minnie and Cassidy seemed to be the outliers. Minnie looked to be in her eighties, while Cassidy appeared barely out of high school. Cordelia gestured toward the empty chair. "Alexandria is here... somewhere."

"She and an older gentleman are arguing in the back of the key room." We all turned to see the waiter, Luca, approach the table, water pitcher in his hand. "From the sound, it's finally winding down."

Pamela made a disapproving sound. "Well... I know it's been a long trip and she's irritated, but I wish she wouldn't take it out on—" She stopped abruptly, her eyes widening, and then she cleared her throat.

Alexandria appeared in the doorway, paused at the soup table to pour a small bowl of stew, and then continued over to take the empty chair. A glance in the other room revealed Angus joining the anniversary party. From up close, Alexandria was even more beautiful than I'd realized.

She sneered at Pamela. "Oh, please don't stop. I'd love to hear the gossip about me firsthand." With a sniff, she stared disapprovingly at Watson, then lifted her gaze to me. "What have they told you? That I'm insufferably selfish? That I made their trip miserable all the way across Kansas because I didn't want them to tag along to begin with?"

"Alexandria," Cordelia hissed reproachfully, while Pamela flinched. "No one said anything. We were just meeting the lovely—"

"Winifred Page, right?" Alexandria cocked a brow. "Can't imagine there're too many other Freds who tag along with a corgi."

"I... am..." I blanched, both from being recognized and for clearly being disdained. "I'm sorry, have we met?"

"No, but I know of you." Once more her tone made clear that whatever she knew about me didn't leave her feeling impressed. But she offered no further explanation and took a spoonful of her stew.

Luca paused with the water pitcher lifted in midair above Pamela's glass and darted his gaze back and forth between Alexandria and me, as if hoping for more drama.

I bit my tongue, refusing to give it to him, and not knowing what in the world I could've done to disgust a person I'd never met.

The rest of the group looked abashed, though none of them were guilty of the faux pas. Cordelia cast another reproachful glance at Alexandria, then refocused on me as she continued to pat Watson. "Well... it was lovely to meet you, and again I'm so sorry we interrupted your party. I promise you we won't be a disruption again."

I glanced back at Alexandria before addressing the kind older woman in front of me. "Not a problem at all. Thanks for being so sweet to my little man here. I'm certain we'll bump into each other again." I started to turn away, then addressed Pamela once more. "I'll make sure to introduce you and Katie."

As I settled back at the table with Katie and Leo, Watson by my side, I couldn't quite get back into the nostalgic, romantic mood I'd been in before. Alexandria had left me unnerved. I had no doubt she knew who I was. Though I'd never seen her, Katie and Anna had apparently, and she had a romantic involvement with Angus, so there were obvious ties to Estes Park. Even so... I couldn't imagine what I had done to cause such a reaction from Alexandria.

Outside the bedroom window, snow streaked by in a rage. There wasn't even a hint of the twinkling lights of Estes Park, not even a glimpse of the tree-tops surrounding us. "I think if we went outside right now, we wouldn't even be able to see our hands in front of our faces. Not to mention that we'd probably be instantly covered with a foot of—" I broke off abruptly as I turned to see a life-sized Cookie Monster on the other side of the room. "Oh... my...."

Katie's smile beamed as her face peered out from under two large googly eyes affixed to the fuzzy blue hood. Some of her brown curls sprang out, hindering the effect, or... maybe adding to it. "You like it?"

Watson growled and backed up, bumping his nub of a tail on the edge of the bed.

"Oh, come on now, it's just me, you big grump."

Katie squatted and held out a fuzzy blue hand. "Smell, I'm still your favorite baker lady."

Watson cocked his head back and forth as if considering, took a step forward, sniffed, and then backed up once more, though he didn't growl again.

"He's probably afraid you're going to try to stuff him in something like that." Without meaning to, I realized I was copying Watson, cocking my own head to the side as I inspected Katie. "Although, you are adorable."

"Yes, I am." Katie straightened. "And I would never force an outfit on Watson. Mainly because I know I'd lose a hand. But I'm glad you approve, because..." She turned and began digging through one of her backpacks.

A sinking feeling arrived in my stomach.

Sure enough, when she turned back around, she held out an equally fuzzy monstrosity, this time in yellow. "I got you one as well."

I gestured down at my own nightgown. "I'm already prepared."

"Not hardly." She tossed it to me, and I caught it on instinct. "Percival and Gary wanted pajama night for the first night. It's their anniversary; we need to make it special."

Holding out the yellow material, I let it unfold,

and a large orange beak protruded from the hood. "I'm *Big Bird*?"

"You're tall." She shrugged. "And yellow was as close as I could get to *mustard*. Be happy I remembered your coloring and didn't dress you up like Elmo."

She had a point there, about red not being my color and about Gary and Percival deserving us to go all out. I began to change into the yellow mess, then paused at a thought. "Oh, good grief. You mean Leo has to see me like this?"

Katie balked slightly, and that time she did an imitation of Watson's head tilt.

Realizing what I'd just unintentionally admitted, I did a quick one eighty as I continued to stuff myself into Big Bird's skin. "So... what's the deal with Alexandria? Granted, my own first impression of her wasn't great, to say the least, but why don't you like her?"

For a moment it looked like Katie wasn't going to allow herself to be sidetracked, but then she plopped onto her bed as she waited for me to change. "She would come into Black Bear Roaster when I worked for Carla. She's good friends with the family. And she's just as condescending and elitist as the whole lot of them. She was almost as bad as Carla's father in treating me like I was dirt under her shoe."

"I can see that. That was how she treated me." I finished zipping up the front of the ridiculous pajamas. "Actually, she treated me a lot worse than dirt under her shoe. I don't think I've ever met her before, but clearly she hates me."

"Well... you and Carla weren't exactly on good terms either, and we know they partially blame you for Black Bear Roaster going out of business. Well... *us*, I suppose." She held up a hand before I could interject. "I'm not saying any of it's valid, but that's their perspective. I'm sure nothing Alexandria's heard from them has been good about you. Not that it would matter. From what I see, she's only friendly to people she thinks she can get something from. Now that I think about it, it's kind of strange that she's part of a knitting club. One, they don't exactly look like her kind of people, and two, the artsy type typically are friendlier."

"Friendly, she isn't." I slipped my hand under my long auburn hair so I could put on the hood without it being in the way. A large beak wobbled in front of my face, and I went a little cross-eyed.

Watson growled again.

I bent down in a flourish and wrapped my arms

around him, pulling him to me. His growling increased, but more indignation at being treated in such an unsophisticated manner than fear of the beak. "Oh, you're fine. Just be glad you get to be pajama free."

I halted at the base of the stairs on our way back down. Once again proving he was more agile than I typically gave him credit for, Watson swerved and darted directly toward the one who'd given me pause.

Leo knelt, and Watson hurtled into him as if they hadn't just seen each other ten minutes before. Then Leo looked up at me, tossed the fuzzy brown elephant trunk attached to his hood over his shoulder —to which Watson didn't even bother to rumble at, much less growl—and grinned.

I smiled back before twisting to glare at Katie. "You ordered Leo's pajamas too, didn't you?"

Katie tapped the side of my head. "Say, it's like you're a real detective. You knew instantly that Leo isn't wandering around dressed like Snuffleupagus of his own accord."

"Big Bird and Snuffleupagus?" I could feel my cheeks heat.

"What?" She simply shrugged and darted around me as if she wasn't in danger. "They go together."

The rest of our party was there, though everyone else had worn normal pajamas. Even the younger nieces and nephews weren't dressed up like Muppets or cartoon characters. It was only a matter of minutes before the blizzard-inducing front door opened once more, and Percival and Gary made their second entrance of the evening. The sight of them made all apprehension of Katie's choice disappear. Gary was clothed in pajamas that looked like Bert while Percival was a too-tall Ernie.

From Katie's gasp of surprise, it seemed she hadn't been aware they'd also been going for a Sesame Street motif.

As soon as they saw us, Percival and Gary erupted in laughter, then the five of us were swept up as everyone began taking photos. Watson, happy for the distraction, wandered over to the hearth of the main fireplace and curled up to sleep.

The waitstaff served steaming spiced cider and hot chocolate and premade s'mores. On the opposite end of the dining room was a long narrow room filled with couches and tables that operated as a library and game room. Most of our party had congregated there. The angst of no internet and wireless seemed long forgotten as my nephews and nieces got lost in a competitive, very loud game of Monopoly with my uncles and Anna and Carl. Leo, Gerald, Jonah, and Noah were at the other end of the room playing a game of cards.

In the dining room, most of the knitting group gathered around Angus, though Alexandria seemed missing. Pamela might've been excited to visit the Cozy Corgi, but the real purpose of their trip was to visit Angus's store, Knit Witt's. He was leading a demonstration of what apparently was an extremely advanced technique.

Katie had talked Lisa into sharing the cornbread recipe, and the two of them were baking away in the kitchen.

Mom, Barry, the twins, and I wandered around in the large room between the library and where Watson continued to sleep contentedly by the lobby fire.

"Look at this one." Mom pointed to an elaborately carved key in a glass case. "Its label says it's from Tibet and is over fourteen hundred years old."

"This one's from Buckingham Palace," Zelda

called out from across the room.

Beside her, Verona chimed in, "And this one is from a castle in Ireland."

The entire room was covered in keys—the walls, the beams overhead, splayed over different cases and stands. Keys of every age, shape, and size. Lisa had finally been able to give the tour of her favorite room when we'd all gathered for the faux slumber party. She'd said that at an official count in 1988 there had been over twelve thousand keys. Since then, several hundred had been added every year. Nearly all of them had tags explaining where they were from. They'd been sent from all over the world, by presidents, celebrities, royalty, and everyday folks who had visited Estes Park. As I wandered around, once more the years folded in and déjà vu washed over me from doing the exact same thing as a child.

"This one was your grandma's favorite." Mom smiled at me as if reading my mind and tapped a three-foot-long key with theatrical mask at one end and an elaborate *E* on the other making up the tines. "It's from the 1920s and was donated by Elitch Gardens, the amusement park in Denver. Mom said she and Dad would go there on dates when they were younger. Quite a drive down the mountain back then."

Barry slipped an arm over her shoulder. "Lotta history in this room. So many lives, so many stories."

It was palpable, a weightiness in the space, but not oppressive. More of a lovely, soft thing. I could easily see why it was Lisa's favorite space in the inn.

I traced one of the nearby letter openers with old-fashioned keys soldered onto the ends. "Maybe Katie and I should leave a key to the Cozy Corgi." I hurried on at Mom's wide-eyed expression. "One of the old ones, before we had the front door locks changed after the break-in."

She relaxed. "I think your grandma would like that." She glanced around, a soft smile playing on her lips as Percival's laugh rang out from the adjacent room before demanding an outrageous amount in rent. "She would like all of this. The family together, happy, safe."

"Oh!" Zelda let out a squeal and motioned for us to join her and Verona. "This is fun and creepy. It's the key to the Stanley Hotel room that inspired *The Shining*."

Mom shuddered and clutched the crystal dangling from her necklace. "I'm glad Percival and Gary wanted to have their anniversary here and not at the Stanley."

"I spent the night at the Stanley once; it's not

haunted. Even did the ghost tour." Barry waggled his eyebrows. "Maybe it was a little haunted."

The Stanley was a huge sprawling hotel on the other side of Estes Park and was the inspiration for one of Stephen King's most beloved novels. "I'm with Mom. I'd rather spend the week surrounded by cornbread, pies, and thousands of keys than murdering ghosts. I've had enough murder for a while."

Zelda waggled her eyebrows in an exact, and probably unintentional, imitation of her father. "Well, the weekend is not over yet."

"Oh, stop it." Verona swatted at her twin, but smirked.

Barry's gaze flitted around the keys and then came to rest on the one from the Stanley once more before his tone grew ponderous. "Maybe that's what Jonah and Noah could do with their shop. One of those escape rooms that are so popular right now. They could design it like Baldpate. Perfect with all the keys."

"Don't you dare suggest anything else to them." All levity left Verona's expression. "I'm ready to murder them both." She shot a look at Zelda, then to me. "You know what? You're right. The weekend isn't over yet. Fred, if you wake up tomorrow and one of them is dead, you know exactly where to look." Without a moment's hesitation, she stormed off.

"Dad!" Zelda gave a reproachful hiss to her father before following Verona.

"I wasn't thinking." Barry looked abashed, and Mom slipped her hand into his.

"What's going on? I've never seen Verona snap at Jonah like she did earlier." I wasn't one to gossip about my stepsisters, even with family, but it was a little off-putting.

Barry shook his head as if in defeat, and Mom answered for them. "Jonah and Noah announced yesterday that they are going to remodel the store another time."

"*Again?*" I couldn't believe my ears. My stepsisters and their husbands had each taken over the two shops on either side of the Cozy Corgi. Verona and Zelda had opened their New Age store months ago. Their husbands seemed close on several occasions but still the windows were papered over. "What is that, the fourth time?"

"The sixth." Barry sighed. "Even I'm getting a little tired of it."

That was saying something. Barry was the most patient man I knew.

"I think I'd be a little frustrated by that myself. In

fact, I'd probably..." We'd walked over to the doorway between the key room and the lobby as we spoke. I glanced over to check on Watson, still snoring away by the fire, but stopped talking as I caught a motion at the bend of the steps. Our server from dinner had been watching us, then darted away.

"What is it, dear?" Mom angled her head to follow my gaze.

"One of the waitstaff..." I had to dig back for his name. "Luca. I think... think he was recording us with his cell phone."

Mom studied the empty spot for a second, then looked back at me. "Why in the world would he do that? Talk about boring subject matter."

"Hey!" Barry reared back and slipped his thumbs into the straps of his fuzzy, oversized, tie-dyed hoodie. "Speak for yourself. I'm an extremely fascinating creature."

With a laugh, they appeared to have shoved the thought away, but I lingered on it for a second. There was a chance I hadn't seen correctly, but I was certain I wasn't mistaken. Maybe Luca hadn't been recording us, but he'd definitely been watching us, and *not* for refills on cider or hot chocolate.

The lobby fire roared, the crackling and popping competing with the raging blizzard outside the windows. Taking a slow breath, I closed my eyes and snuggled deeper into the cushions of the overstuffed sofa.

Everyone else had gone to bed less than ten minutes before, and Lisa had stoked the fire for me before she'd gone up. I had yet to open the book on my lap, relishing being alone, save for the warm weight of Watson as he napped on my feet. As much as I loved my family and friends, I'd discovered long before that I required time alone in order to recharge. If I'd simply gone upstairs and fallen asleep at the same time as Katie, I'd have woken the next morning exhausted, no matter how much sleep I might've gotten.

Letting the wind and the fire soothe, I opened my eyes, smiled lovingly at Watson, and finally cracked open the latest installment of Kelley Armstrong's *Rockton* series. It was a little bit mystery and a little lost in the wilderness, and it seemed perfect for the weekend. Despite the sensation that Luca had been observing us earlier, I settled in between the barely glowing lights of the key room and the glassed-in porch, and felt nearly as safe and cozy as I did in my own home, or in the mystery room at the bookshop.

Grabbing a piece of the cakelike cornbread I'd snagged from the kitchen, I chewed happily and made it about halfway through the first chapter before a squeak at the stairs caused me to flinch.

Watson lifted his head, giving a sleepy growl. It faded quickly, as he was able to see into the dark stairwell more easily than me.

After a pause, there was another squeak, and Carl Hanson came into view. He gave a little self-conscious wave. "Well... Fred and ah... Watson." He glanced behind, clearly considering retreat. "I didn't realize anyone was awake."

"Just catching up on some reading." I knew it was horrible of me, but I so hoped Carl didn't decide to sit down and chat.

He didn't, instead rushing toward the kitchen. "Anna... wanted a snack."

Relieved, I gestured toward the plate of cornbread on the coffee table. "Help yourself to these. Katie and Lisa made it, so they're fresh, even a little warm still."

Another hesitation and then he came forward. "Sure, you don't mind?"

I held them out to him. "Honestly you'd be doing me a favor. If you don't take them, I'll eat every single piece."

"Perfect. Thank you." After taking them, he headed upstairs.

I turned back to the book, but before I reached the second chapter, the front door of the inn opened, ushering in snow and wind. That time Watson's growl didn't stop when the person came into view, though it wasn't overly aggressive.

Gerald shut the door and stamped the snow off his boots before noticing the two of us and giving a little jump. "Oh! I didn't expect anyone to be awake."

Déjà vu. Might as well go with it. "Just catching up on some reading."

"Good idea." Gerald cleared his throat and gestured

back to the door. "I was just... I had... um..." With a flick of his hand, he appeared to give up and headed toward the stairs. "Well, have a good night, you two."

For the billionth time, I wondered how in the world the man experienced any success at all as a lawyer. "You too, Gerald."

I stared after Gerald though he'd disappeared, tracing Carl's footsteps into the dark. Both men had been acting strange, somewhat guilty. Carl often acted strange, but *guilty*? Not so much. Perhaps he hadn't been getting a snack for Anna after all. Seemed like a coincidence that he and Gerald would be up and about at the same time. Probably another kombucha run, though surely Gerald had that in his room, not in his car.

Letting it go, I turned back to the book, allowing myself to get lost in the comfort of the fire, and made it nearly to chapter five before the combination of Watson snoring and the white noise of the blizzard outside began to lull me to sleep.

Another creak at the steps shot me awake once more. Though it had the same effect on Watson, that time he didn't growl.

I was starting to feel like I was in the middle of Grand Central Station. Considering I'd just seen

Carl and Gerald, chances were high it was Angus, the third of the kombucha buddies.

It wasn't. And by Watson's lack of a growl and the happy wagging of his nubbed tail, I should've figured it out instantly. That time, Leo emerged from the stairs. He smiled in surprise. "Hey, you're awake." There was no hesitation or guilt in his tone.

"Thought I'd just do a little reading." Third time's a charm. "But it was about to turn into napping."

"Well, I don't want to disturb you." Despite his words, he hesitated. "I was having trouble sleeping, so I thought I might peruse the little library, see if there was anything good."

His hesitation was clearer than Carl's and Gerald's, and my heart began to pound, a spike of adrenaline clearing out any notion of sleep. I gestured to the other side of Watson. "Go grab a book, and you can join us, if you want."

"Okay. Sounds nice." He smiled, but instead of heading toward the key room and the library behind it, he walked around the coffee table and joined us on the couch. Proving just how tired he was, Watson didn't do a happy dance, but whimpered contentedly as Leo's fingers sank into his fur, and pressed his head against Leo's thigh. Leo cooed something nonsensical to him and sighed. "This is nice—the fire, even the storm outside."

I couldn't help myself. "You didn't get a book."

He chuckled softly. "No, I suppose I didn't. But I can. We can just sit and read. We don't have to chat."

If it had been anyone else, even Katie, I would've taken that offer. But the idea of talking with Leo, though both exciting and uncomfortable in ways, was about as far from draining as I could imagine. "No, let's chat."

Another smile, and a nod. Leo opened his mouth and then closed it once more, apparently not sure what to say.

Neither was I, and I was suddenly aware I'd not taken off the Big Bird onesie Katie had stuffed me in, but at least I didn't have the hood on and a big beak sticking out over my face. Of course I'd find myself seated on the couch with Leo, by a fire, and dressed in fuzzy yellow. I went with it. "I can't believe you changed out of your Snuffleupagus pajamas. That trunk looked unbelievably comfortable."

Leo snorted, and some of his ease returned. "I think now I know how people with long hair feel. I had to keep flipping it over my shoulder like it was the world's longest ponytail."

"True, but most of the time ponytails don't come out of the center of your forehead."

He graciously chuckled again at my poor attempt of a joke, then fell silent. I could see the awareness in his eyes, even from the flickering light of the fire. I'd been certain, but was even more so in that moment—he'd sensed the change in me, felt an unspoken awareness that we weren't just friends, not really.

I cleared my throat. "So... how was... um... time with family?" I grasped the lowest hanging fruit I could reach, and I regretted it instantly. Leo wasn't overly secretive, but he never said much about his childhood or provided any details that were too specific about his mother or siblings.

"Oh. Fine. It was... fine."

Sure enough, that had been a wet blanket. I tried to think of something else, but nothing was coming.

He twisted suddenly, angling more toward me while never losing contact with Watson, and his demeanor changed. "Actually, it was rough. Exhausting, really. It's good to be back."

The abrupt shift in his tone surprised me, and I realized that this too was a change, an opening up, a risk. "I think a lot of people experience that during the holidays. Even though my family is pretty wonderful, with so much time together and all the parties and events, it can leave me a little desperate for an opportunity to close the door and shut out the world." I started to leave it at that, but then decided to go a little further. "Want to share what made it stressful?"

Leo was silent for a while, but I got the sense he was debating *how* to say it, not *if*. Finally he sighed again, like he was giving up a little bit. "Without getting into all the details, as that's really not what I want to dwell on right now, let's just say I'm starting to realize I simply have to accept my family is who they are. I keep hoping for more growth, more progress, but..." He shrugged.

Once more unsure what to say, I decided to try to make him laugh. "You mean like all of us hoping that at some point Barry will wear something other than tie-dye?"

It worked. A soft bark of a laugh erupted from him. "Yes, exactly like that." And though his chuckle faded away, Leo seemed lighter again, even as he went deeper. "I wish it was that. My father was a pretty... despicable guy. To Mom, to us kids. And being the oldest"—another shrug—"it was my job to keep everybody safe, at least as much as I could. Mom included."

He had never spoken that clearly, but it matched

the impression I'd formed from the few things he'd said, so I nodded in understanding. "Your dad's out of the picture, right?"

"Yeah. Since I was sixteen." He nodded and sighed again. "But in ways, it's like he never left. Or at least that everyone still fulfills the same roles they always did." He held my gaze. "Mom sees herself as a victim. Instead of my father, it's everyone. Her boss at work, the guy in front of her in the grocery store checkout line, the lady who delivers the mail. She's constantly waging war with everyone. Except... for the landlord who is horrible to her. Except for the pastor at her church who tells her she needs to work on the marriage with my father even though he's been gone for nearly two decades, because marriage is forever. Except with my little brother who lives two blocks away and has apparently decided he wants to fill in Dad's old shoes." He looked away, focusing on Watson. "To *those* people, Mom's still a victim. And she won't hear a word against any of them."

Once more I didn't know what to say, and after a moment's hesitation, I leaned forward and slid my hand on top of his where it had come to rest on Watson's hip.

His bright eyes lifted to mine once more, and

when I didn't pull away, I saw things in the depths that he'd only allowed me to see flashes of now and again since the day we met—flashes I'd ignored or shoved off as something else.

When he spoke, his words were thick with emotion, but the corner of his lips curved into a soft smile. "One of the things I've loved..." He flinched as if he just shocked himself, then after a blink, shook his head and met my eyes again. "No, I'm just going to call it like it is. I could say one of the things I've admired about you, and that's true, but it doesn't really capture it." He moved his other hand, covering mine so it was sandwiched between both of his. As if he was giving me time to pull away, he didn't speak for a few seconds. When I didn't, his smile grew. "It's one of the things I've loved about you from the day we met. You're strong, Fred. You came barging into the national park with that owl feather, determined to find answers, and you haven't stopped since. It doesn't matter if you're in danger or if people tell you to mind your own business. You're nobody's victim. You're nobody's fool."

I could barely breathe from the sincerity and admiration in his gaze. I wanted to argue. After Branson, I'd very much felt like I'd played the fool. Just like I had with my ex-husband and my ex-business partner.

"You're just the opposite. You fight for people who are victims, for truth. I have seen you weather bump after bump over the past year... more than a year... that we've known each other. Bumps and betrayals, things that would flatten other people, and you... just keep going. And you don't get hard because of it, either."

"Leo... don't..." Even I could barely hear my whisper.

"Sorry. I said too much." He started to pull his hand back.

I gripped it, holding him in place so we were ridiculously stacked like a tower on top of Watson. "No, it's not too much, not like that."

When his gaze lifted once more, there was hope there.

Maybe we'd already crossed a line we couldn't go back from. Probably had. Maybe, for him, that had happened the night he'd given me the silver corgi earrings. Maybe, for me, that moment on Christmas Day at Hidden Valley.

"Not like that." As I repeated it, I moved my thumb over the back of his hand. "I just don't deserve the praise you're heaping on me. You're sugarcoating it all. I'm bullheaded, sometimes too aggressive. I demand too much from—"

"Don't do that." His voice was firm, but there was no unkindness in it. "That's exactly what I'm talking about. Those descriptors you're trying to put on yourself right now? They're from what everyone else says Winifred Page should or shouldn't be. But even so, you charge right ahead, and even when you're not entirely sure of yourself, you're always who you are."

I couldn't help but laugh at that. "Well, that's true. For better or worse."

"Exactly." He nodded. "Exactly. And it blows my mind every time I get to see it."

My eyes stung suddenly. I wanted to tell him everything I admired about him. How I'd come to depend on his friendship, his strength, his goodness. How his stabilizing force had made the past few months bearable. Without him there were times I would've crumbled. But I didn't trust my voice to attempt to speak.

He didn't offer me the chance to, anyway. He took his top hand off mine and lifted it to my cheek, his thumb stroking it as I had the back of his hand, and he leaned nearer, his gaze refusing to let me look away.

We stayed like that for several moments. The light of the fire flickered over the right side of his face as his left was awash in the cool bluish gray from the snow whirling outside the window.

No, there was no coming back. Even if we stopped right there, right then, things would never be the same again, if they'd ever had any chance of it anyway.

If I'd planned it, I would've taken longer. Maybe weeks, maybe months, taking little bitty steps. Or knowing me, one step toward him and then five back. But I'd been doing that since the day I met him, hadn't I? Even though I'd not been aware of it.

Before I could second-guess, before I could list all the reasons we needed to slow down and not go from the pace of molasses to the speed of lightning, I covered his hand with mine and leaned nearer as well so we were mere inches apart. "Kiss me."

A laugh broke from Leo once more, one that sounded of happiness and relief. He cut off the sound as he pressed his lips to mine.

In the moments I'd let myself consider this possibility, I feared that when we finally gave in to what had slowly built between us, our lips would touch and we'd discover we really were just friends after all, that there would be no spark, just the cold affection of relatives, or something equally as horrible.

They'd been wasted worries.

A sigh escaped, but I wasn't sure if it was from me or him. Leo's hand slipped from my cheek and moved through my hair until he cupped the back of my head and deepened the kiss.

I didn't know. Maybe sparks flew, maybe the earth shook. Possibly, as there was a loud pop from the fire. Or... maybe none of those things happened.

Either way, my world shifted. Perhaps that had been part of why I'd refused to even consider the possibility for so long. Leo Lopez was dangerous. There would be no coming back from him, and some part of me had always known that. Things would never be the same.

Between us, Watson gave an irritated huff and hopped off the sofa, his hind legs sliding behind him like a seal's tail as he plopped to the floor.

Though we both chuckled, neither of us broke the kiss, and Leo drew himself nearer, his other arm slipping behind my back and pulling me to him until he was cradling me against him.

I didn't know how long the kiss lasted, nor how we shifted positions. But at some point his back was against the arm of the sofa and I was cradled between his legs, my head resting on his chest as his fingers played through my hair.

Watson sat below us on the floor, snoring softly.

Neither of us spoke for a long time, just settling into this new strange world. But that was the weird part—it didn't feel strange. It just felt... right. Natural.

After a while, I tilted my head slightly to kiss him again, right as there was a gasp from across the room.

Watson barked, and Leo and I jerked apart.

"Oh my goodness, I'm so sorry." Lisa Bloomberg stood at the base of the steps, her hand covering her mouth. "I didn't think anyone would be up."

I started to pull farther away, but Leo laid a hand on mine as he chuckled self-consciously. "It's okay."

Lisa pointed above her head. "I woke up and walked to the bathroom, but the lights wouldn't come on. I thought I'd check the breaker." She pointed again. "I can go back up and—"

"No. It's totally fine." It was my turn to laugh. I glanced toward the key room and the glassed-in front porch. "Huh, I didn't even notice the lights go out." Maybe the loud pop hadn't been from the fire after all.

Lisa hurried around the fireplace, flicked on the flashlight on her cell phone, and disappeared behind the counter. There was a metal scrape from what I assumed was the fuse box, then a few clicks. When she emerged, she was shaking her head. "No power at all." Without waiting, she crossed to the glassed-in front porch where we'd celebrated the anniversary only a few hours before and peered through. "It's hard to tell, given the blizzard, but I don't even see a faint flickering of a light from downtown. Looks like the power is out everywhere."

Over the next half hour, we helped Lisa retrieve lanterns, candles, and matches from a back room, lit our own, and then dispersed others in front of the bedroom doors so people would have them in case anyone else woke up in the middle of the night.

We said an awkward goodnight to Lisa, and then we were standing in front of Leo's door, Watson at our feet, only our two lit lanterns illuminating us.

Leo cupped my cheek as he had downstairs. For the first time, there was a sliver of nervousness in his tone. "Are you okay? Freaking out a little bit?"

I started to shake my head, then paused, doing a quick self-assessment, wanting to be truthful. "Actually, I'm not freaking out. I know I should be."

"I'm not either." The nervousness left his voice. "And why should we? We're not teenagers. And while this aspect might be new, *we* are not. I know exactly who you are."

Save for a few details, like the ins and outs of his family, I knew who Leo was as well—at least the core of who the man was.

He kissed me again, long, sweet, with an undercurrent of fire. Finally, he pulled away.

There was that moment. We'd already darted across so many bridges, I could slip into his room and cross another.

For whatever reason, that felt too soon.

"See you in the morning?" Whether he'd read my feelings or was having the same himself, there was no sound of frustration or disappointment. Only happiness, and a contented quality that I'd never realized had been missing from Leo.

"Yeah." Maybe it was too soon, but I was disappointed, pleasantly so. "See you in the morning."

Another kiss, and then Watson and I walked a few feet to Katie's and our room, turned to give Leo a wave, and disappeared inside.

SEVEN

I shot up, sitting straight in my bed, trying to figure out my surroundings. There'd been a noise. Someone was in the kitchen.

Watson grunted as the bed squeaked. His scowl was barely visible in the dim light when I looked over the side of the bed. Then he rested his head over his forepaws once more with a grunt.

Only then did I realize we weren't at home. But I couldn't quite place it until I looked across the room and saw Katie sleeping soundly.

Right. Baldpate. The anniversary party.

Good Lord, I had to be completely exhausted if I was that out of it. A glance at my cell phone revealed it wasn't even four in the morning. No wonder.

I peered out the window. The storm was still blowing, nothing visible but gray streaks of snow, and even that was hard to see.

My head almost reached my pillow when I shot back up again, this time fully awake, my heart pounding. And *not* because of any sounds in the night.

The memory of Leo and me in front of the fire crashed back into view.

For a moment or two, there was nothing but pure, unadulterated terror.

What had we done?

What had *I* done?

Had we really jumped from being friends on the drive up to Baldpate Inn to... to... whatever this was, in a few short hours?

Another noise sounded from somewhere outside my room, distant and muffled. I barely noticed it. Probably just something from the wind outside, or someone going for another midnight snack.

Just as I began to struggle to catch my breath in my panic, I felt Leo's hand on my cheek, remembered the sincerity in his honey-brown eyes as he spoke of all the things he loved about me. My body relaxed as I exhaled, and my lips tingled with the ghost of our kiss.

I slid from the bed and sat beside Watson, put my arms around him where he lay, and folded over him.

He merely grunted once more, an annoyed indulgence.

His warmth, his constant presence, grounded me, lessening my panic the rest of the way.

Maybe Leo and I had skipped over several steps in one big leap, and sure, such recklessness wasn't like me, but that was all protocol. We'd been building up to this for over a year, even if I hadn't let myself realize it. And besides, every other thing in my life I'd planned methodically. Step by excruciating step. My degrees, my first marriage to Garrett, opening the publishing house with Charlotte. And look how they had all turned out. There'd been one other time where I'd simply closed my eyes, tossed caution to the wind, and leapt. That spur-of-the-moment decision had brought Watson and me to Estes Park to open the Cozy Corgi. And *that*, without a doubt, had been the best decision of my life.

Fear gave way to peace. And in a matter of a heartbeat, peace gave way to anticipatory excitement. Everything was going to change, but it was right. I could feel it, and just like on the snowy slopes of Hidden Valley, just like on the couch in front of the fire, further puzzle pieces snapped together, erasing all doubts. Things falling into place, even if I couldn't quite see the final image.

I pressed a kiss between Watson's ears. "At least I know you approve." I nearly laughed at that thought. As if there was going to be anyone in my life who didn't approve of Leo and me. And like I'd change anything even if they didn't.

After a few more seconds of snuggling with Watson, I stood, intending to get back into bed, but couldn't make myself. I was wide-awake, despite barely any sleep. I was too excited, too happy, too... everything.

I'd go back down, grab another piece of cornbread, relight the fire in the hearth, and read. Or at least pretend to read. I'd probably just sit there and glow.

I snagged the lantern I'd left beside the bed, crossed to the door, and slowly turned the handle so it didn't squeak. I intended to let Watson sleep, but he popped up and followed me the second I moved into the hall, his nails clacking softly over the hardwood. After shutting the door once more, I lit the lantern, and then Watson and I made our way to the stairs, only pausing by Leo's door. I touched the old smooth wood, letting my hand rest there for a few moments.

Finally.

The thought surprised me. I hadn't realized I'd

been waiting. I didn't think I had been. But the sensation was true enough. There was excitement, anticipation, butterflies, but woven through everything was a sense of relief. Contentment.

Dropping my hand, we continued to the steps and made our way down, a few squeaks here and there.

There was another noise from somewhere in the dark. It sounded like it was over to my left, toward the key room. Goose bumps prickled on my arms, threatening the warm peace that had been cascading through me. I attempted to shove the unease aside.

Watson didn't help by issuing a low, warning growl.

"It's okay. The inn is over a hundred years old, and we are in the middle of one of the worst blizzards I've ever seen. There's going to be strange sounds," I whispered to Watson, but I might've been reassuring myself more than him. The lobby was notably colder than the few hours before, a frigid draft blew over my legs from under the nightgown I'd changed into before crawling into bed.

Instead of going to the kitchen first, I knelt in front of the fire and pulled logs from the stack on the hearth.

Watson growled again, and I looked over to see

him with his ears pointed back and his head low to the ground as he crept toward the key room.

I stood instantly, clutching one of the pieces of firewood in my right hand, just in case I needed a weapon. There was no reason to try to reassure myself or Watson that it was the settling of the old hotel. By that point, I more than knew Watson's growl—I should've recognized it the first time, should've realized from the prickling of my flesh.

Lifting the lantern, I took a few steps forward, the candlelight only illuminating the first few steps into the key room.

Watson trailed beside me, his continuing growl low but steady.

I stopped a few feet into the key room and chastised myself. This was hardly our first rodeo. I might know what we were getting ready to find, but I had no idea what situation we were about to walk into. There was no reason to do it on my own.

However, just as I turned around, ready to go wake up Leo, Katie... everyone, that very thought forced all caution to the wind. My entire family was under this roof; it could be one of them.

I hurried forward, swinging the lamp from side to side, the candlelight casting bizarre and jagged shadows from the thousands of keys. It was hard to tell in the dimness, but nothing seemed out of place. The farther we went, the stronger the icy draft became. At the far end of the room, the door swung slightly on its hinges. It was the source of the cold, and it wasn't a draft—it was a breeze. Watson and I increased our pace and paused only when we reached the doorway into the library game room. I peered in. Sure enough, the other door at the opposite end of the long narrow room also swung on its hinges, ushering in the cold, wind, and snow from the outside.

Watson's growl transitioned from low rumble to full-on warning agitation, and he slunk farther into the room.

I nearly called him back, but fear over who I'd find pressed me onward as well.

From what the lantern light revealed, everything looked the same as it had earlier that night. We'd nearly reached the door to the outside before the shadowy figure came into view. It was male, clearly, but I couldn't tell much else in the flickering shadows. He lay partway behind an old armchair, sprawled on the floor. The pool of blood was inky black in the darkness, flecks of snow whipping in through the door and covering it, only to melt instantly.

Dropping the piece of firewood, I rushed toward the body, some part of my brain screaming that with that amount of blood there was no way the person could be alive. Even so, I didn't pause as I reached the prone form. With panic rushing through me, I grabbed an arm, experienced a bit of hope feeling the warmth of the skin, and rolled him over.

All hope vanished at the sight of the slit throat.

I had to hold the lantern right by the face before I realized who it was.

Luca. The handsome young German waiter.

Maybe it was horrible to admit, but relief so strong flooded through me that I nearly collapsed. So great, that I had to reach behind me and steady myself by gripping the back of the armchair. He wasn't family, wasn't a friend.

Watson's snarl pulled me back to the moment. He was standing in the doorway, growling out into the stormy night.

Moving around Luca, I hurried toward Watson and slipped my fingers into his collar, lest he decided to give chase. Holding my lantern out past the door revealed nothing. There was only darkness and swirling snow. The moonlight barely broke through the swirls. A glance down didn't even expose footprints. In whatever time had passed, though it couldn't have been much at all, snow was already piling in a heap through the doorway, covering any tracks. Only then did I notice an old-fashioned key partway between the growing mound of snow and the pool of blood. I repositioned the lantern once more, causing the key's tarnished pewter to glisten. Not just a key, but one of the letter openers I'd noticed earlier in the evening. Blood glistened over its sharp blade.

EIGHT

Tears brimmed in Lisa's eyes, but I was impressed at how well she pulled herself together. She bent, reaching lovingly toward Luca's soiled face, but she caught herself before I could tell her to stop. Standing, she wiped the tears from her eyes. "Guess I shouldn't disturb Luca's body."

"No, we need to leave the scene as close to how we found it as possible." Never mind that I had already turned over the body, but that couldn't be helped. My gaze flitted from Leo and Katie to my mom and Barry. All of their faces were tense and strained in the light of our lanterns. They were the only ones I'd woken up. "The first thing we need to do is alert the police. I tried dialing 911 before I got any of you. I'd forgotten the phones don't work."

"I can run out to my Jeep and see if I can get anyone on the..." Leo's words faded away, and he shook his head. "Right... I rode up with you and Katie. No CB in the Mini Cooper."

Katie's brows furrowed. "I can't believe I'm suggesting this, but doesn't Susan—?"

"I just don't understand who would do this to Luca." The words burst from Lisa, and fresh tears finally began to fall. "He is a..." She scrunched her eyes closed. "He *was* such a sweet boy. So full of life. I can't accept that anyone would..."

Mom moved closer and put her arm around Lisa. She didn't say anything, just held her supportively.

Watson paced the room, sniffing the path we'd taken over and over again, every once in a while disappearing into the key room and then returning again.

"Come here, buddy." Barry knelt, holding a hand out to him and then patting his head comfortingly when Watson came. To my surprise, Watson only indulged Barry for a moment or two before taking off once more, sniffing around as if his life depended on it. Barry's gaze traveled after him as Watson disappeared into the key room again. "Looks like Watson's already on the case. I'd wager he'll have it figured out in a matter of minutes." He chuckled as he stood once more.

"Barry," Mom whispered scoldingly.

Barry cleared his throat self-consciously and looked to Katie. "You were getting ready to suggest contacting Officer Green, I believe."

Watson's growl drew all our attention to the doorway before Katie could respond.

A soft muttering followed, only increasing Watson's irritation.

Before I could make it to the doorway, two women peered in, the lantern they held illuminating their faces in a ghostly uplight. They were from the knitting group. I couldn't remember their names, but one of them was the youngest member.

The older spoke. "I heard noises, so I woke Cassidy. I have trouble sleeping anyway because of the knee replacement I had last year. It aches something awful all the time. But this cold is making it worse." They entered the room, still not able to see Luca's body from that angle. "Goodness. You are quite the partying lot, aren't you? Have you even gone to bed yet?"

The younger woman, Cassidy, it seemed, yawned and then motioned upward. "We discovered the noise, Betsy. Are you satisfied? Can we go back to bed now?"

Watson was still sniffing around their feet, the rumble in his chest continuing, and then, giving a sharp bark, he darted back into the key room once more.

Leo shot me a glance and headed toward Cassidy and Betsy. "Why don't you come with me and we can—"

"Lisa!" a girl's voice sounded from somewhere in the shadows.

Watson let out another bark.

"Lisa?"

"Oh no." Lisa sucked in a gasp. "I didn't even think." She pulled away from Mom and headed across the room.

"Lisa?" The girl's voice sounded panicked.

"Lisa? Are you back there?" A male's voice, sounding more annoyed than worried.

"Hold on. I'm coming."

Though Lisa called out to them, the two hurried into the back room, joining our small crowd, Watson on their heels.

Two of the waitstaff, though I didn't remember their names either. As soon as he noticed the group gathered, the man halted, but the girl hurried forward when she saw Lisa. "We can't find Luca. He was supposed to stay with me last night, and I woke up and realized he wasn't there. I must've fallen asleep... but... I went to his and Beau's room, and he—"

Even as her eyes went wide and her words fell away, Lisa took the girl by the shoulders, attempting to spin her around and lead her away, but it was too late.

The girl jerked free, stumbling toward Luca's body. Lisa was able to regain her grip and pulled the girl close, stopping her before she got any closer. For a few seconds, the girl stared in confusion, then horror washed over her face, and she began to scream.

Within a matter of minutes, nearly everyone was gathered in the lobby. Someone had lit the fire, but I wasn't sure who. The girl, whose name turned out to be Juliet, had screamed and screamed and screamed, waking the entire inn. Her screams had given way to sobs that wafted through from the other side of the fireplace where the staff lounge was hidden. Lisa had left her with Beau and the rest of the young staff who'd come downstairs at the commotion.

The rest of us, now joined by Zelda's and Verona's families, the Hansons, Angus and Gerald, and Minnie, the eldest member of the knitting group, gathered in a misshapen circle, some of us seated on the sofas, some standing, while others paced. The only ones not accounted for were Percival and Gary and four others of the knitting club, as they were all staying in the smaller cabins outside the inn.

I'd taken a seat on the floor, directly in front of the spot Leo and I had occupied on the sofa only a few hours before, making room for the others. Watson plopped at my side, sitting at attention, pointed ears twisting back and forth at every noise.

"So one of us is a murderer." With the roaring fire and all the lanterns lit, the wild expression over Anna's face was crystal clear. "And we're stuck in the middle of the forest, during a blizzard, without any contact to the outside world, without any electricity. We don't have any heat even. So not only are we at the mercy of the elements, but we've got a crazed killer among us."

"Anna." Noah was reproachful as he spared a glance toward his children, then glared back at Anna. "Let's not slip into dramatics. The fire is plenty warm, and we're not on the set of a horror movie."

"Aren't we?" Anna went shrill, gesturing toward the key room and library. "We've got a dead boy bleeding all over the floor. *That* would say otherwise."

"I have to agree with my wife." Though Carl's tone was icy serious, the flicker in his eyes revealed that he was enjoying the excitement. "It could be anybody. *Any* one of us."

Murmurs broke out among the group at that, while the members of the knitting club looked terrified, and Lisa appeared nearly sick to her stomach.

"Enough!" Leo's voice cut through the chatter. "This isn't helping. Noah's right. We're not in some slasher flick." He swung his gaze toward Anna, anticipating her interruption, and cut her off at the chase. "But you're right as well. Clearly *someone* killed Luca, but that doesn't mean it was someone within these walls. And even if it was, it hardly indicates a killing spree. There's no reason to believe anyone else is in danger. Either way, panicking isn't going to help."

While I hadn't even come close to slipping into a panic, my thoughts had been more along the lines of Anna's—instantly wondering who among us had killed Luca. I'd already taken out half the suspects. No one who'd come for the anniversary party would do such a thing. Of course. I couldn't imagine anyone from the knitting group doing it either. Once before I might've excluded the possibility simply because most of them were older women, although I'd learned the hard way that just because someone looked like a grandma didn't mean they weren't a murderer, but still. Why would one of them drive across the country, arrive in the middle of a snow-storm, and kill one of the employees of the hotel?

That left the owner, who looked grief-stricken as she stood by the fire. Or one of the other young people who were currently comforting the still-wailing girl.

"Susan Green lives pretty close, right, Fred?" Katie was finally able to finish her thought from before. "We might not have phone service or elec-tricity or anything, but we could drive to Susan's house. She might have power, or at least a way to get in contact with the station."

"That's a good idea. I was preparing to suggest that myself." Gerald had been about to lift a bottle of kombucha to his lips but lowered it once more. "As a lawyer, I have to stress the importance of getting law enforcement involved as quickly as possible." His gaze flitted to me. "The murder scene has already been compromised."

"Oh, Gerald." Mom gave a similarly reproachful tone to the one she'd used with Barry earlier, though it was harsher. "What did you want Winifred to do? *Not* check to see if she could help the poor boy?"

"Now, Phyllis, don't get riled. Clearly, with his throat cut, the boy was beyond—"

Angus put a restraining hand on Gerald's shoulder from where he stood beside him, but didn't bother to address the sentiment, instead looking toward Katie. "Have you looked outside? There's not a car up here that will make it through the snow. It's up to my midthigh."

"I have two snowmobiles. They're in good working order." Lisa sounded exhausted, her voice faraway. "I need to call Luca's parents. I wonder what time it is in Germany. I've never had to..." Her words trailed off as she shook her head. "Oh... Right. No phones."

Mom went to Lisa again, attempting to comfort her.

"That will work. I'm good on a snowmobile. We use them in the park all the time," Leo spoke up, decisively.

"You're not going on your own." Katie gestured toward the window. "It's still storming, and if it's too dangerous to drive, then—"

"I'll go with him." I spoke up before I'd even thought it through.

Leo smiled knowingly at me. "Have you driven a snowmobile before?"

I lifted my chin. "No, but... I can figure it out."

"This depth of snow isn't the time to try to learn, dear," Barry interjected. "I'll go with you, Leo."

I could see Mom start to object, but she stopped herself.

"Besides..." Leo crossed the space between us and knelt down to look me meaningfully in the eyes as he stroked Watson's head. "You've got a job to start, don't you?"

"A job...?" His meaning clarified instantly, and I couldn't help but chuckle. "I'm sure Susan will appreciate that when you bring her here."

He shrugged. "Maybe not, but don't you think she'd be disappointed if you didn't give her something to complain about?"

Gerald put down his kombucha bottle once more. "Now listen here. I know Winifred has solved more than her share of—"

"Good idea, Leo." Once more, Angus stopped his friend before he'd barely gotten started. I decided Gerald was a lot more palatable when Angus was around. He looked to me. "I'll help you any way I can, Fred. I'm sure we all will."

Most of our rather large group nodded along. I

was a little taken aback both by the assumption that I was instantly going to start looking into who killed Luca and by the show of faith they had in me. For a split second, I started to deny that I was going to try to figure out what happened, then didn't see the point. Hadn't I already been crossing off suspects in my mind? And really, by this point, it was just what I did. And if there was ever a murder that justified me looking into it, it was this one—shut off from the rest of the world with no police involved.

I glanced out the window, then back to Leo. "It's probably still an hour and a half before sunrise. You should at least wait until then."

"We'll be fine." He paused for a couple of moments, his gaze holding mine. Even in the midst of what was going on and all the people around us, I could see the memory of the night before flicker behind his eyes, and I thought maybe a question as well, wondering if I was regretting, having second thoughts, or about to panic. Then it was gone. "Besides, by the time Barry and I bundle up and we get the snowmobiles running, it'll be that much closer to sunrise. And with how heavy the blizzard still is, the sun won't make that much difference anyway."

With that, it was decided. Leo and Barry went

off to put on as many layers as possible. Jonah and Noah moved a sofa in front of the doors to the key room, marking it off-limits. And Lisa vanished behind the fireplace to comfort the rest of her brood of employees.

Watson was nearly beside himself watching Barry and Leo disappear into the dark swirl of snow, barking furiously from where he, Mom, and I stood on the deck overlooking the parking lot.

Mom glanced at him in concern and then toward the path Barry and Leo had taken. "You think Watson knows something? That they shouldn't go?"

Though I was worried as well, I couldn't help but chuckle. "No. That's not his warning bark. That's his offended *why are you leaving me when I want to play* demonstration."

Sure enough, Watson barked again, bounced up and down on his short stubby front legs, eliciting a small avalanche over the side of the porch.

"Never mind that half the time he puts one paw out in the snow when we're home and decides he's too delicate for such weather, but if it's Barry and Leo, he's ready to be strapped to a snowmobile and tear through a blizzard."

Mom studied him and finally gave a little chuckle of her own, looking relieved.

Unable to help myself, I stared off once more to where they'd disappeared. What little I could see of the forest was so dark and mostly obliterated by the whorls of snow whipping around. I had no doubt Leo knew what he was doing. As a park ranger, he'd done more than one rescue mission in bad weather conditions, but I didn't know if they had been as intense as this. Would it really have made that much difference to at least have waited until sunrise?

After a few moments, I felt Mom's gaze on me and looked over to her.

She cocked her head, and then a knowing look entered her eyes. "Oh. Something's changed, hasn't it?"

I flinched, feeling like I'd been caught red-handed at something. "What do you mean?"

She only smiled and patted my hand. "That makes me happy." Another pat. "Don't worry. Our men will come back to us."

Juliet's sobs had lessened to sniffles and ragged breaths by the time Watson and I made our way to the other side of the fireplace. Beau remained by her side, holding her hand. Lisa had gotten the rest of the staff preparing breakfast. It would be mostly leftovers and cold items, but there was an old wood-burning stove they'd kept for appearances that they were attempting to put back into working order.

With one hand in the young man's beside her and her other stroking Watson's head, Juliet looked at me in sad confusion. "So... you're a detective or something? You going to question us?"

"No." I tried for a soothing smile. "I own a bookshop downtown. But I've helped solve a few murders in the past, and my father was a detective, so I'm aware of some of the protocols. But... you are, of course, under no legal obligation to speak to me at all. I simply wanted to ask a few questions about last night, about Luca." As I said his name, Juliet's tears increased. I decided to use her emotion over the boy to my advantage. "I hope I can help get justice for Luca as quickly as possible."

"Okay." Sniffing, she nodded and pulled her hand from Watson long enough to wipe her eyes, not that it did any good. "What do you want to know?"

"If I understood you correctly, it sounded like Luca was supposed to spend the night with you?"

Another nod.

I spared a glance toward Beau beside her and

then back to Juliet. She'd said she wanted him to stay, so apparently there weren't any secrets between them. "Does that mean you and Luca were... romantically involved?"

She nodded again, and her tears increased.

Beau slid his free arm over her shoulder, pulling her close tenderly, and kissed the top of her head as he murmured gently. The familiarity of the gesture caught me off guard. It seemed more than what a friend would normally do.

Maybe...

I refocused on Juliet. "Were the two of you keeping your relationship a secret?"

"No." She spoke in a questioning way, as if unable to imagine why they would. "Luca didn't have secrets. He doesn't believe in them."

The memory of him videotaping Barry, Mom, and me the night before flickered in my mind. I highly doubted Luca didn't believe in secrets, but he most definitely didn't believe in privacy. "And you said he was supposed to spend the night with you last night?"

"Yeah. It was our night together. But I hadn't slept very well the night before." Juliet struggled to take a breath and then pushed on. "Maybe if I hadn't fallen asleep, I would've realized something was wrong."

"Juliet, it's not your fault." Beau pulled her closer once more. "I didn't notice Luca hadn't come back to our room either, like he normally does before he goes to you."

"Oh, you and Luca were roommates?"

"Kinda." Beau offered a partial shrug and met my gaze for the first time. His eyes were nearly as red and puffy as Juliet's. "We are roommates, but more than roommates."

"He and Luca were dating as well." Juliet squeezed Beau's hand, clearly trying to comfort him.

"You and..." My brain short-circuited as it tried to do the math and couldn't. Then studying Beau's arm over Juliet's shoulder and where their hands were clasped, I thought I did. "So the *three* of you were dating?"

They both shook their heads. But it was Beau who answered, and Juliet's tears increased once more. "No. *We*"—he gestured with a nod toward Juliet—"were both dating *Luca*."

I thought I knew the answer but pushed ahead for clarification anyway. "Luca was dating both of you, and you both knew it?"

Once more that look of bafflement crossed Juliet's face. "Of course."

"And you were okay with that? Both of you?" I didn't have a problem with how people chose to live their lives, even so, this particular concept baffled me a little. "And were the two of you dating as well?"

"No." Exasperation filled Beau's voice, slipping into a quality as if he was explaining the obvious to a five-year-old. "*Juliet* was dating Luca, and *I* was dating Luca. Juliet and I are not dating. We're just good friends. Everyone knew; everyone was okay with it. It's just like Juliet said earlier. Luca didn't believe in secrets. None of this was secret, not from any of us."

Juliet scrunched up her nose, considering. "I don't think Lisa really caught on."

I knew I was pushing things, given Beau's irritation. However, I wasn't sure if he was growing short with me because he felt it should all be obvious, or because I was barging in on things he didn't want me to know. A little further push might answer that question. I leveled my gaze on his. "Do you *want* a romantic relationship with Juliet?"

The genuine grimace that crossed his expression left no doubt about his sincerity. "No. She's my friend. That's it. I have *no* interest in girls. Not that way. I loved Luca."

"Oh, Beau." Juliet started sobbing again and wrapped herself fully in Beau's embrace.

I blinked, trying to sort it all out. Attempting to connect their relationship to Luca's murder. Perhaps Beau was done sharing Luca with anyone else. Although if that was the case, wouldn't he have killed Juliet? Something about that didn't sit right, and both Juliet's and Beau's affection felt genuine. But... complications in romantic relationships were frequent motives, so... maybe...

NINE

"Good morning! Hope you're all ready for day two, because we've got a bunch of..." Percival burst through the front door of the inn, Gary directly behind him. He scanned the lobby. His gaze flitted over our group, which was gathered around the sofas arranged in front of the fireplace, then traveled over to where most of the knitters clustered in another grouping of overstuffed chairs. Some were knitting, others simply looked shell-shocked, probably wondering what they'd gotten themselves into. Percival's cheerful expression fell. "Good Lord, this is a celebration, and you all look like you've gathered for a funeral. Who died?" He attempted to crack a smile but didn't quite make it.

"One of the young waiters." Mom spoke up from where she was braiding Christina's hair. "Luca."

Gary's eyes went wide, but Percival's narrowed.

"Oh, don't be..." His words trailed away as his gaze landed on me. "Fred... really? This weekend of *all* weekends?" He flung open his boysenberry-colored fur coat, revealing a glittery T-shirt. "I ordered my Barbara and Judy outfit special."

Despite the heaviness that had settled over the hotel, I couldn't hold back a squawk of a laugh. "Me? *I* didn't do it!"

Percival propped a bony hand on his hip. Before he could argue, Gary gave him a nudge, but addressed me. "And we know you'll solve it as quick as that." He snapped his fingers.

"I think I'll go back to our cabin, sit in the whirlpool until this is over, even without the bubbles." Percival wheeled around. "Let me know when the party mood returns."

Gary rolled his eyes and put a hand on Percival's shoulder, holding him in place.

"Seriously, Percival. Don't you think you're being a little callous?" While she reprimanded her brother, Mom glanced over at the group of knitters, clearly embarrassed to imagine what they were thinking.

"After this happening so many times, it's hard to —" A fresh wail of sobbing filtered in from another room. Juliet would do well for a while and then launch into hysterics once more. Percival glanced toward the sound, then sighed as he blushed. "Good point. He was a handsome, charming kid, if I recall. The blond German young man, right?" When I nodded, Percival sighed again and took the empty place on the arm of the sofa. "Let us know how we can help."

Lisa emerged from the dining room, holding a large pot of coffee. "Breakfast is served. It's been a while since we've had to use the wood-fired stove, so it may not be quite up to snuff." She gestured with her head toward the dining room where two other members of her staff—neither of whom I recalled from dinner the night before—were carrying heaping trays. "But it's warm, and I'm sure we all could use it."

Watson had been napping by the fire, but at the scent of food, he perked up and barely spared me a glance before springing off the hearth, shooting like a bullet to the dining room.

Katie chuckled beside me. "I love that little guy. Good to know there's a few things in life you can always depend on."

"Yeah." Percival's mutter was barely audible. "A chubby dog who likes food, and a murderer to ruin every party."

"Percival!" Mom hissed at the exact same moment Gary elbowed him.

As our group and the knitters started to wander into the dining room, Lisa pulled me aside. Katie hung back with me. "Do you mind if Kelvin and I speak to you for a second? He's just informed me of some things I think you ought to know." She glanced at Katie, eyes narrowing in slight distrust. I was sure it was weird enough to be talking to a bookseller about a murder, let alone her baker friend.

Katie didn't seem the least bit offended and smiled at me. "I'll make sure Watson doesn't eat his weight in carbs, and I'll fix you a plate as well."

Lisa motioned toward one of the vacated sofas, and I followed her over. It'd been a little over an hour and half since Leo and Barry left. The sun was coming up, brightening the whirling snow outside the windows. We'd barely gotten seated before one of the servers who had been delivering breakfast came in.

"Winifred, this is Kelvin." Lisa gestured toward the young man, then prodded him gently. "It's okay. Just tell Ms. Page what you told me. It's better to get it all out in the open."

He gulped and met my gaze but then darted away quickly. "I... ah..." He shook his head.

I stayed silent, unsure what to say.

After a few moments, his dark eyes flashed at me. "I didn't hurt Luca." He had a thick British accent.

"Okay. That's good." I attempted an encouraging smile. "Anything you can tell me may help."

Kelvin fell silent again.

I heard the clacking of Watson's claws on the hardwood before I saw him waddling into view, peering around questioningly, and then his brown gaze landed on me, clearly wondering why I wasn't at breakfast. To my complete shock, instead of hurrying back to the food, he plodded over and plopped down at my feet with an annoyed sigh.

A partial smile flitted over Kelvin's lips as he watched Watson, and then he looked back up at me. "I couldn't stand the bugger, but I didn't hurt him. No matter what they say."

"Okay, I believe you." Maybe I did, maybe I didn't. He sounded genuine enough, or at least genuinely angry enough even in those few words. If he'd truly killed Luca, surely he'd try to do a better job covering his dislike. "And no one has told me anything about you yet."

"I know. I already asked Juliet and Beau what they told you, so I figure it's better for you to hear it from me, before one of the other snitches blabs."

Kelvin glanced down at Watson again and then unleashed. "Luca was an obnoxious git. Constantly filming everybody on his stupid cell phone and then lording it against us. Last week he caught me..." His cheeks reddened, and he glanced at Lisa, who nodded. After considering for a moment, Kelvin continued again. "Well, let's just say Luca was threatening if I didn't do the things he told me to, he'd post it online."

"What did he tell you to do?"

Kelvin reached down and started stroking Watson, his gaze following the movement, and he seemed to become more at ease.

He shrugged. "Nothing horrible. To do more of his job responsibilities while he napped or messed around with Beau or Juliet. Had me buy him cigarettes when we went into town. Junk like that, but I was already getting tired of it. We had a big blowup two days ago, so..." Another shrug.

"So you're worried people will think because of what he was doing, because of your fight, that I'll think you killed Luca."

He nodded.

Lisa jumped in. "I thought I'd put a stop to Luca's videoing months ago. He fancied himself a documentarian." Kelvin snorted at that, but Lisa kept going. "I le was applying to some film schools. I knew he had been filming some of the staff without their permission, and I caught him filming me once, nothing incriminating or embarrassing, just going throughout the normal routine. He *never* did it to any guests. If he had, I would've had no choice but to let him go." She cringed. "Although, maybe I was wrong about that. I thought he'd stopped altogether. I shouldn't have trusted him."

"Nah. Not your fault. You're just good-hearted. You treat us all like you're our mum." The affection Kelvin felt for Lisa was clear, and matched the impression I had of her. "Luca was good at deceiving people."

I did believe Kelvin. He seemed forthcoming and open. And while I didn't think he'd been the one to murder Luca, he'd opened another possibility. Maybe Luca had caught another member of the staff in a moment serious enough they were willing to kill over it.

Watson perked up, gave a happy bark, and then bounced onto the sofa, standing on his hind legs so he could look over the back and see out the window. A second later, I heard the reason why. The faint sound of engines, then silence.

"Leo and Barry must be back." I stood and

offered a hand to Kelvin. "Thank you. May I come to you if I have any more questions?"

He shrugged again. "'Course."

When footsteps sounded on the stairs outside, Watson hopped off the sofa with another happy yip, ran to the front door, and began spinning in circles in pure delight. I knew at the end of the day I was the one Watson loved, *his* human, but I never stopped marveling at the reaction Barry and Leo prompted in my cantankerous little corgi.

When the door opened and the first person stepped in, Watson stopped halfway through one of his happy spins and growled.

"Trust me, fleabag, you're not who I wanted to see either." Officer Green ripped off a wool cap, her brown hair loose and messy instead of in the typical short tight ponytail she normally wore. Her pale blue gaze found mine. "You just can't help yourself, can you?"

I let out an exasperated huff. "As I've already said, *I* didn't kill anyone."

She smirked. "Whatever you have to tell yourself to sleep at night, Angel of Death."

Leo and Barry followed behind her, reigniting Watson's joy to nearly astronomical levels as they both knelt and simultaneously lavished attention on him.

Within a few minutes, Barry, Leo, Katie, Lisa, and I were gathered at the far end of the library game room.

Susan had been asking questions as she snapped pictures of the scene and jotted notes. She'd finished a few close-ups of the key letter opener and turned to me. "So your primary theory right now is that our victim here spied on the wrong person. You're dismissing the love-triangle aspect?"

I waited for the punchline of Susan's question, she sounded as if she genuinely wanted my input. When it didn't come, and I was silent for an awkward amount of time, she prompted with a cocked eyebrow. "Yes. It doesn't make sense, and I don't think Juliet is capable of killing someone." From my peripheral, I noticed Lisa nod her agreement. "I'm leaning toward his spying and filming habit."

Susan considered, looking down at Luca's body once more. "You may be right. Whoever did this was most definitely not happy with him."

Again I waited for a punch line. But it didn't seem like one was coming. Maybe things really had changed between Susan and me. She was treating me like my theories held water. Not only that, but there hadn't been one comment about me sticking my nose anywhere it didn't belong.

"I suppose the good thing, at least for the moment, is that all of our suspects are contained." Susan opened the back door before looking at me. "Although, you said this was open when you came in?"

"Yes. But they could've easily circled around and come back in through another of the doors."

Lisa chimed in, "There are also four smaller cabins on the grounds, three of which are in use at the moment."

"There's always the possibility it's somebody who's not staying at Baldpate." Leo shrugged when Susan gave him a doubtful stare. "Maybe, it's not likely, especially considering the weather, but the way it appears, maybe this kid had romantic entanglements in town, or was attempting to blackmail someone else."

"During a blizzard?" Again Susan sounded skeptical. And once more threw me off. I was used to that tone with me, not directed at Leo. Though, there was none of the scorn that typically went along when she addressed me.

"I'm not saying it's likely, just that we need to

consider all possibilities." Leo grimaced. "We also need to figure out what to do with Luca's body. He's stayed there too long as it is."

I glanced toward Susan, then back at Leo. "What do you mean? Now that Susan's here, the rest of the authorities can't be far behind."

Barry shook his head. "Turns out, things are worse than we realized."

Susan bugged her eyes out at me. "Maybe you haven't noticed, with your nose in a book and in other people's business, but there's the blizzard of the century going on outside." *There* was the annoyed, condescending tone I was used to. It was almost reassuring. "No one is going to be joining us here today, maybe not even tomorrow. It's almost like a disaster area out there. I shouldn't have come home last night. It took me hours. By the time I considered turning around, I'd already gone halfway. By this point it's a billion times worse." She studied Luca's body as she spoke. "There's no power in town at all. Last communication I had, they still weren't sure how many lines were down. Trust me, short of a tank, there's no car or vehicle that's going to be able to come up here anytime soon."

It was hard to imagine the whole town without

power. "But we can't leave Luca like this. Surely helicopters could—"

"In case you didn't notice, Fred. He's as dead as he's going to get. It's not exactly an emergent situation." She sounded like she was enjoying herself. *Yes, still Susan.*

True to form, I felt my own tone take on a condescending quality. "In case *you* haven't noticed, the murdered body indicates a murderer. And while Leo's theory might be right, it's a very good possibility that whoever killed Luca is still here with us."

Susan groaned. "Great, so now you're going to turn this into a serial-killer type of situation? Who's the next victim?" She raised a finger. "Wait, wait, let me guess. It's the fat dog, with a knitting needle, in the kitchen."

"Breathe, Susan." Leo gave her a reproachful glance, then turned to me, his tone softening. "From what Susan's been told, there was a mass pileup late last night on Highway 34, and a rock-and-snow avalanche in the canyon as well. All available emergency crews, including helicopters, will be dealing with them for the foreseeable future, as those take precedence since there're lives that may need saving."

I was struck dumb for a moment at the thought

of it all. Estes Park sounded as if it had transitioned from magical little village contained in a snow globe to disaster area. "That's horrible."

Susan looked over at Lisa. "Now there, we're all caught up. We do need to move our victim's body. I'm assuming your refrigerators would be large enough to..." She shook her head. "No electricity, but they should stay cold for quite awhile."

A look of horror crossed Lisa's face.

Susan didn't notice and kept going, talking to herself as she glanced out the window. "The snow would be better, but out in the open like that..."

"There's an old icehouse." Lisa sounded sick to her stomach, growing pale as a sheet. "It used to be..."

Katie put a steadying hand on Lisa's arm. "It's okay. This is awful, but you don't have to face it alone."

Susan nodded, moving along. "An icehouse will work. We'll just—"

"Hey!" A shout from the other room caused us all to turn. "Give that back."

As one, we all hurried from the room. As we entered the key room, I saw Beau chasing Watson, my little guy's eyes wide with fear, and something gripped in his mouth.

I rushed toward Beau and grabbed his arm. "What do you think you're doing?" I didn't bother to worry about how tightly I squeezed when I jerked him to a stop.

He flung out a hand toward Watson, who'd taken shelter behind a large showcase filled with key paraphernalia. "He's got Luca's phone."

"What?" I looked at him like he was crazy.

"His phone." Beau gestured again, but this time over to another case by the entrance to the key room. "He was snuffling behind that, then popped out with Luca's cell phone in his mouth. When I tried to get it, he tore off."

"Tied." Leo's voice drew my attention. He was kneeling beside Watson, comforting him with one hand and holding up an iPhone in a red case with his other.

I shot a glare at Beau before going to Leo and Watson. I knelt down and took Watson's face in my hands, pressing my forehead to his. "It's okay, buddy. You're a good boy. You're a good, good boy." He was trembling. Watson might not be the biggest people person, but he wasn't used to humans acting aggressively toward him, either.

Leo spoke again before I could give in to my own

murderous thoughts. "There's something sticky all over it."

"Probably that dog's spit." Beau spoke up from behind me, and I whirled around just in time to see him snatch the phone from Leo's hands. I was about to launch into him, but the expression that crossed his face held me back—a little jolt of surprise, followed by a quiet gasp that sounded part pain and part fondness. "I think it's cookie dough." A small smile turned the corner of his lips. "Luca was always sneaking into the refrigerator, stealing cookie dough."

As I continued to stroke Watson, I made a mental note to get him a piece of that cookie dough. Even if it wasn't good for dogs, or anyone else, for that matter. My poor little guy just thought he'd found a delicious snack and then got chased all over the room for it.

Not swayed by Beau's emotion, Susan stomped over and plucked the phone out of his hands. "Is this what Luca would spy on people with?"

Anger flitted over Beau's face, but he nodded.

Susan tapped the screen and let out a frustrated grunt. "Passcoded."

"I'm not giving it to you!" The angry words burst from Beau.

He tried to snatch the phone back, but Susan

yanked it out of reach. "Calm down. I didn't even ask you to." She considered and looked at me though she spoke to Beau. "*I'm* not in the place to ask you that."

I caught on instantly. She couldn't demand anything without a warrant. With the final scratch on Watson's head, I stood, channeling my anger to something productive. "No one can make you give the password up, Beau, but the fact is, someone killed Luca. Probably someone within these walls right now. And unless you're the one who did it, I'd think you'd want to help solve his murder. You *claim* that you loved him."

He glared, fury radiating from his eyes. "I did love him. I *do*."

Maybe Leo was feeling the same as me because when he gestured to the phone, his voice was hard. "Then prove it."

"Beau, please." Lisa came up, speaking in a motherly tone and attempting a reassuring touch.

He shrugged her off, sneering. "What do you expect to find on here anyway? You think he recorded his own murder?"

Susan looked at him with all the disdain she typically saved for me. "Are you afraid he did?"

Beau's face grew so red he looked like he would pop. Then with a curse, he yanked the cell from her grasp, punched his finger repeatedly against the screen, before thrusting it at me.

When she hesitated, I took it. "Good choice, Beau. This might help Luca."

He didn't reply, but a tear made its way down his cheek.

Before he could change his mind, or the lock-screen returned, I found the camera app and went into the photos and videos. Everyone except Beau gathered around, watching over my shoulders. I tapped the most recent video and felt my heart lurch.

It was nearly too dark to see, but from the angle, it looked like Luca had been spying from the corner of the glassed-in front porch to the strip of parking below. He was zoomed in on one of the vans the knitting club had driven—the back doors were open, and there were two figures unloading something.

Gusts of gray snow obliterated the entire scene for several moments, and Luca's whispered curses cut out the sound of the wind.

The figures returned to view and fluttered out again.

They came into view once more. One figure remained shadowed in the back of the van, another moved a few feet away, holding something.

"Is that...?" Katie nudged closer, her whisper brushing against my neck.

Before she could finish the thought, the figure looked up, searching as if knowing someone was watching, then looked directly into the camera.

Luca cursed again before the figure took off, heading in the direction of the stairs up to the inn. The image vanished in a blur and a loud crash. It took a second to realize Luca must've dropped the phone. He picked it up with yet another curse and then, from the motion and sounds, ran.

The video stopped.

I turned to look at Katie. "Alexandria."

She nodded.

TEN

"Alexandria?" Susan snatched the cell out of my hand and reversed the video a few seconds, squinting at the screen. "Alexandria who?"

"Uhm..." I racked my brain, trying to recall if I'd heard her last name. "I'm not—"

"Bell," Katie piped up, but her tone wasn't bright, as it normally was when she answered a question.

Susan's eyes narrowed further, then widened. "You've got to be kidding." She glared at Katie, then me, as if it was our fault. "Alexandria Bell is here, seriously?"

I pointed toward the dining room, though from where we were, we couldn't see in. "She came with the group of knitters."

Without another word, Susan turned on her heel and stomped off across the lodge. As she moved, she dug a band out of the back pocket of her slacks and twisted her hair into her trademark short ponytail.

Katie and I, and the rest of the group, exchanged looks and followed her.

"Where is she?" Susan hadn't finished stepping up to the table full of knitters before barking out the question.

The six women looked over at her, startled. The one who'd bonded with Watson... Cordelia... gave a quick once-over at Susan's uniform, sat up a little straighter and lifted her chin. "Where is who, Officer?"

"Don't play games. And don't try to cover for her, or I'll—"

I hurried to the table, Watson by my side. It seemed Alexandria had the same effect on Susan as she had on Katie—more so, actually. "We're looking for Alexandria." I shot Susan a warning glance, for all the good it would do, and then addressed Cordelia. "We have a few questions about... what she might've seen last night."

The fancy blonde, Pamela, gasped and lifted her fingers to her throat. "You don't think Alexandria had anything to do with that poor boy, do you?" She cast a quick look around at the other women, then addressed me instead of Susan. "I mean, she can be harsh, judgmental, and a little... superior, I suppose, but surely she wouldn't murder someone."

"Of course not." Betsy shuddered and her weathered hand reached over to pat Cassidy's beside her. "We'll never get the image out of our heads. Alexandria might not be the most pleasant, but she couldn't do something like *that*."

"We're not at liberty to discuss any matters of the case at this time, and we're not asking for theories." Susan's impatience was palpable, but she did seem to attempt a more cordial tone. "I simply asked her whereabouts. Are others of your group absent this morning?"

"No, the rest of us are here." Cordelia spoke smoothly and more calmly than her sister. She also appeared more curious than anything else. "I'm afraid we wore out our welcome with Alexandria when we invited ourselves along on this little adventure. She—"

"I wouldn't put it like that." Pamela spoke up again. "We didn't *invite* ourselves. We merely—"

Cordelia silenced her with a look and then turned back to us. As she spoke, Watson padded over to her and received a scratch on his head for his efforts. "She needed some space from us and has her own cabin. I'm sure she's still sleeping."

"I placed her in the twin sisters' cabin." Lisa had joined us at the table and addressed Susan. "She requested lodging that was the farthest away."

"Typical." All attention turned to the oldest member of the group. She sniffed primly, though her eyes looked bloodshot and the tip of her nose a bulbous red. "She's a little snooty, that one."

"Minnie." Pamela gasped once more. "Really, she's not even here to defend herself. There's no need to—"

"I've met Alexandria on more than one occasion. Snooty is apt, I'd say." Pamela was cut off again, this time by Susan. "Not to mention, arrogant, entitled, rude, and downright annoying."

The entire table, even Cordelia, looked somewhat shocked at Susan's declaration, all except for Minnie, who tapped the end of her red nose with one finger and pointed at Susan with another. "Good discernment is an honor to your badge." Minnie leaned forward, speaking directly to Susan. "Good thing you're here. I don't know what all happened last night, but every few seconds, there was the creaking and moaning of floorboards in the hallways, and every time I looked out, there was someone or other sneaking about. It was like everyone in the inn had somewhere else to be than tucked in bed like proper people." Her bloodshot gaze flitted to me, held, and looked away. She sniffed once more. "Murder wasn't the only scandal occurring during the night."

I felt my cheeks heat. Maybe she'd heard Leo and me walking back up from our time at the fire. Had she seen us hesitating by his door? I hadn't felt anyone's eyes on us, not that it mattered. Although, she had a point. I'd noticed myself that it seemed there had been a lot of movement in the middle of the night.

Surprisingly, Susan didn't seem to notice Minnie's accusing stare and turned to Lisa. "Take me to her cabin."

Lisa only hesitated a moment before she nodded and started to turn away, but then Cordelia spoke up again. "Perhaps you'd like me to come with you. It might go easier if you have someone Alexandria knows."

"I'm more than capable of doing my job. Thank you." Susan barely spared Cordelia a glance before motioning Lisa onward.

I gave an apologetic wince toward the table, then followed Susan and Lisa, Watson hurrying to catch up when I was a few paces away.

We hesitated long enough by the check-in

counter for Lisa to grab a jacket. Barry started to ask Susan something, but she shushed him. In surprise, I realized I knew Susan well enough by this time to recognize she was coming up with a plan. From her growing scowl, it appeared she wasn't overly fond of whatever scheme she was hatching. Finally she turned toward our group, pointing to Leo. "You, come." Her finger moved to me, and she hesitated a moment longer. "You as well. Go get your jacket." She turned to Katie and Barry. "You two stay here. I don't need the entire Scooby Gang. Besides, you can both keep your eyes on those knitting women. I don't trust anyone who has nothing better to do than sit around all day twisting fabric together."

Within a matter of minutes, Lisa led Susan down the steps of the inn and then toward a path that was nothing more than a gap in the trees, considering the depth of the snow that wound up the steep embankment. We passed a couple of other cabins, and Leo and I trailed behind. Watson, proving once more that as long as Leo was present he was in heaven, trundled through the snow without a complaint, one moment barreling along underneath the thick white blanket like a groundhog and the next bounding through it as much as his tiny legs could bound through the tracks we left behind.

Though I couldn't tell from the flakes, I got the sense that the blizzard was waning somewhat, more from the increasing brightness than a lessening of the snowfall. I was thankful I'd abandoned my broomstick skirt in the room as I grabbed my jacket, trading it for snow pants and winter boots, as the snow came up to midthigh in several places. The wind had died down, allowing the snow to fall in a way that didn't smack into our faces. Outside of the crunch of steps and the rustle of our clothes, the world was an oddly muffled silence. If I didn't know how destructive it had been in Estes Park and the canyon, not to mention walking in on a murder that morning, I would've found it beautiful, maybe the most beautiful winter landscape I'd ever seen, completely otherworldly in a way.

Even the sound of Susan pounding on the door seemed faraway. When there was no answer, she glanced at Lisa. "You brought your keys?"

Lisa nodded, suddenly looking nervous again. "I did, and I'm sure you're clearer on the laws than me, but I can't unlock her door unless you have a warrant."

Susan had already started to knock again and paused with her hand still raised. "I wasn't suggesting—"

The click of the deadbolt cut her off, and a second later, Alexandria's pretty face glared through a crack in the door. "What is it? I don't like to be..." Her words fell away as she noticed a small group outside her door.

"Alexandria Bell?" Susan's tone took on a distant professional quality.

Alexandria focused on Susan, studying her with an expression that suggested she recognized the police officer, but wasn't entirely sure who she was. "Yes?" The word came out questioningly, and then, as if not liking the sound of it, Alexandria straightened, opened the door a few more inches as her tone took on a defiant quality. "Yes, I am she. Who are *you*, and what do you want?"

"I'm Officer Green. A young man was murdered at the main lodge sometime in the night or early this morning." Susan delivered the line without a shred of emotion, then waited.

Alexandria barely missed a beat. "That's terrible." She spared a glance toward Baldpate, then at the rest of us before looking back at Susan. "What do you need?"

Her response surprised me, no emotion was evident in her voice or flooded over her face. She didn't even bother feigning concern.

"I need you to come back to the lodge. I have some questions for you." Susan gestured at the gap in the door. "Or you can invite us in."

Alexandria bristled. "As I said, that is terrible, but I don't appreciate my privacy being interrupted. Nor your implication that I might be involved in anything to do with such unsavory events."

"I wasn't implying anything." A slight enjoyment seeped into Susan's voice. "However, we do have a video shot by the deceased, which very clearly shows you and another person out in the middle of the night loitering at the back of one of the vans."

The twinge in her eyes was barely noticeable, if I hadn't been inspecting her, I would've missed it. "I'm sorry, is there a curfew in Colorado mountain towns that I'm not aware of? Is it illegal for me to be outside of my cabin after a certain time?"

The corner of Susan's lips curved slightly. "So you're not denying you were meeting with someone in the middle of the night during the worst blizzard we've seen in years?"

Alexandria's chin lifted even further, and she stood a little straighter, the door opening a little more at the motion. "Again, is there a curfew or some other Podunk law that I've unintentionally violated?"

"From the training I've received, Ms. Bell,

murder is against the law, regardless if you find the locale to be Podunk or a metropolis."

Alexandria rolled her eyes, and instead of seeming offended, shifted to uninterested. "Really? I'm a suspect in a murder? What did I do? Kill someone, then saunter back here, light a fire, and curl up in bed?"

"That's what I'd like to ask you about." Susan took a step back, the heel of her boot bumping against Watson's leg. Though he chuffed in protest and moved out of the way, Susan didn't look down. "Would you like to invite us in or return to the inn?"

"Actually I didn't sleep very well last night. I'm going back to bed." She started to shut the door.

Susan moved again, bumping into Watson once more, that time with a touch more force. Her movement cutting off Watson from Leo and me.

Before I could protest, Watson, completely irritated and cut off by Susan's legs, took his only escape route and darted through the door of the cabin.

Alexandria let out a startled cry and then cursed angrily. "Get your nasty animal out of my room. He's dragging in snow and goodness knows what else."

Susan pushed open the door and gestured through. "You heard the woman, Fred. Go get your fleabag." Though I'd been about to reprimand

Susan, there was a quality in the look she gave me that helped me realize she was up to something. "Leo, why don't you help her? The last time that dog did this, someone got bitten. I don't want to add that paperwork on top of what I already have to do."

Trying to control my irritation and confusion along with my expression, I walked in past Alexandria, Leo behind me. The entirety of the small cabin was visible from the doorway. Directly in front was a large restroom, to the left a bedroom, and to the right a large family room with a fireplace. Watson sat in front of the hearth, glaring.

I started to say something to Leo, then noticed Alexandria giving us a glare of her own.

Not sure what Susan was up to, I attempted my best guess. "You're making him uncomfortable. Would you mind giving us a little space? Watson has anxiety issues."

"*Anxiety issues?* For crying out loud," Alexandria practically hissed.

"They need a little room." Leo casually put his arm over Alexandria's shoulder, angling her away.

Alexandria twisted free, then whipped around to face Leo, venom and fury dripping. Not that I could blame her for a man she didn't know to be acting so familiar. "If you touch me again, I'll sue you for assault."

"Listen, lady." Leo held up his hands. "I'm not trying to assault you or anything. Just hoping to keep you from getting bitten by a dog. I only wanted to—"

Alexandria hissed out something else at him, but Susan's quick motion at the inside door handle behind Alexandria caught my attention. She pulled her hand back and her eyes met mine. "Hurry it up, Ms. Page. We don't need any more drama today. Can you get that dog out of here, or do I have to call the pound?"

Both somewhat impressed with what had just gone down and irritated that she'd used Watson in such a manner, I bent down and wrapped one arm around Watson while slipping the other under his chest and belly to give support, whispering by his ear before I lifted him up, "Sorry, buddy. I promise I'll make this up to you."

Watson hated being carried and played the part of crazed dog perfectly by thrashing in my arms. He was heavy enough, I nearly dropped him and had to hold tighter, which only made him writhe more. It was enough to pull Alexandria's attention away from Leo as Watson and I squeezed past them and out the door.

Susan pointed to the far side of the cabin. "Take him over there, keep him far away from Ms. Bell and the rest of us."

Through it all, Lisa stared wide-eyed at the display. From her expression, I got the sense that she too knew something was going on more than met the eyes but wasn't sure what. I didn't think she'd noticed Susan messing with the door.

Leo followed me out, sidestepping Alexandria and joining us in the deep drifts of snow by the cabin. As soon as I set him down, Watson darted a couple of feet away, clearly feeling betrayed, only to have a large embankment of snow crash down on him. Leo came to the rescue, shoving the snow away, then plopping down to cradle Watson in his lap.

Instantly soothed, Watson snuggled up to Leo while casting glares in my direction.

I refocused on the scene in the cabin doorway just in time to hear the end of Alexandria's accusation. "If it was some kind of ploy to get into my cabin, Officer, I promise you, I'll have your badge. I have connections to this town that will—"

"It's a dog, Ms. Bell," Susan interrupted, and though her voice was loud, her tone remained bored. "An ill-trained, annoying one at that. I can promise you, it has no association with the police department or me. If it did, I'd be the first one to toss the fleabag in a sack and launch it over the nearest bridge."

Even as my temper spiked hearing such words from Susan, despite knowing they were merely a means to an end, I couldn't help but be surprised at Alexandria's revolted expression. "You really are as awful as I'd heard."

To my further surprise, Susan flinched, as if stung. She gathered herself quickly enough. "Your personal opinions of me, or other people's for that matter, are of no consequence. If you don't want us to come in, then I invite you, once more, to join us at the main lodge."

Alexandria opened her mouth, her impending refusal clear, but Lisa broke in. "We have breakfast ready, and coffee. It's hot, and I think we could all use a little caffeine, don't you?" She actually smiled at the woman. "And I'm so sorry this is happening during your visit. Believe me, I'll make it up to you. How about a weekend, all-expenses-paid stay here, in the cabin of your choosing?" I was impressed with the innkeeper's quick thinking.

"You think I'd ever stay here again?" Alexandria sounded disgusted, but relaxed somewhat at Lisa's offer and her tone. Finally, with a glare at Susan, she nodded. "Fine. Coffee it is. Wait while I slip into something warm."

Before she could shut the door, Susan took a step forward, one foot in the doorjamb.

Though she glared, Alexandria disappeared from view, I assumed to get dressed. Within a minute or two, she was back, clothed in an expensive matching fur jacket-and-boot set. She shut the door, cast another glare toward Watson, Leo, and me, and then stormed off toward the main lodge, leading the way as if it had been her idea.

As soon as they were out of sight, Leo stood, Watson cradled in his arms, content as a baby. He grinned at me. "Come on, let's see what we can find."

ELEVEN

For a few moments, I stared dumbfounded at Leo's retreating back as he carried Watson toward the cabin, glancing from him to where the three women disappeared. It was almost like Susan and Leo had rehearsed.

Realizing I was playing the part of a fool by standing out in the snow, I hurried after them. Leo had already placed Watson on the floor of the cabin and held the door open for me, then closed it once I stepped inside. "Did you and Susan go over possible scenarios while driving over on the snowmobiles?"

Leo gave me a puzzled look, then gestured to the door. "You mean this?" He shook his head. "How could we? Alexandria wasn't a suspect in my mind. And I didn't even think about telling Susan she was here, although, I didn't know they knew of each other."

"It's like you two were reading each other's minds." Somewhere in there, I reprimanded myself. It didn't matter, at least not in the moment. I needed to search Alexandria's cabin, figure out the how and why of it all later.

Leo's puzzled expression shifted, growing darker somehow, and his tone became more concerned. "Remember, with all the poaching stuff and the rest of the police department and..."

I sighed when he paused and forced a smile. "It's okay. You can say his name. We have plenty of times before."

"True enough." He swallowed and nodded before charging ahead. "When Branson and the rest of the police wouldn't take my concerns about the poaching seriously, Susan did, or at least tried to. There were a couple times she looked into things with me behind their backs." He shrugged, then gestured to the door again. "As far as this, Susan couldn't search the cabin without a warrant, but you and I can. Well..." He gave a dark chuckle. "I guess not really, but more than Susan. I figured she needed to make sure the door wouldn't lock when it was closed. And it's not like you and I haven't done this kind of thing before."

As soon as he said it, things clicked, and I was

able to label my ill-at-ease moment. Yes, we had done it before. Here we were again.

I heard more than felt the brush of Watson's fur on my snow pants and looked to see him staring up at me. He gave a questioning whimper and an expression that read, *What in the world is wrong with you? This is Leo. He's better than treats!*

Before I could reassure or even mentally answer my perceived question, Leo stepped nearer, gently taking me by both arms and holding me lightly until I met his gaze. "I'm not Branson, Fred. I don't have a secret life. I don't have a different name. I'm not involved in any criminal activity. As you know, I have a past, a past that has me mostly comfortable in situations like this. I figured we'd get to them over time, but if you need all the details, we can sit down right here and right now and go through every one."

He hadn't even finished his little speech before I was breathing easier. He'd labeled that too, but it had merely taken looking into his eyes for a few seconds for me to rest assured that while I may not know every in and out of Leo's life, I knew who the man was, the real man. And part of him knew how to break into a house, and another part of him both understood and was okay with searching someone's cabin while local law enforcement turned her back.

His thumb rubbed gently over my shoulder. "If you're not comfortable with this, we don't do it. That's not a problem."

I considered for another moment. I couldn't help but think about what my father would do in this situation. He'd been, like Susan, part of the law, and I couldn't imagine him doing this. Though I was certain there were things I didn't know about his career and choices he'd had to make on the job. And what was more, my father wasn't there in the cabin with us. I was definitely my father's daughter, but I was also my own woman. And maybe this had shades of gray, but we were in special circumstances; we needed to know who the murderer was. All signs indicated Alexandria had been the last to see Luca alive. Somehow it felt right, but we needed to be sure. "No, I'm okay with this. Let's see what we can find."

With a smile and a minuscule nod, Leo dropped his hands from my arms.

I grabbed one of them, catching his attention once more. "*And* I know you're *not* Branson. I trust you. And I don't want to hear everything in one big explanation like it's a confession or something. We'll get there when we get there."

Leo relaxed a little but stayed serious. "Okay. If

you ever change your mind, let me know. There's nothing I won't tell you, even the shadowy stuff."

The urge to kiss him washed over me, it almost made me laugh. Such a strange new development, but I shook both impulses away. "All right, let's do this. Though I have no idea what we're looking for." I refocused on Watson again, who was now seated at our feet, looking back and forth between the two of us. "You found Luca's cell phone. Can you find anything tying his murder to Alexandria?"

Proving that whatever we were looking for wasn't covered in smudges of cookie dough, Watson didn't tear off to uncover all the answers in the corner of the room, merely sat there, tongue lolling happily as he basked in the presence of two people he adored.

The thought made me laugh, and I bent to pet him. "Looks like you've forgiven me, by the way. I really am sorry that I picked you up and—" Before I could touch him, Watson chuffed, scooted toward Leo, and pulled his tongue in, giving me a serious expression. "Spoke too soon it seems."

Leo chuckled and nudged my arm. "What do you think? Divide and conquer?"

"Sure." I scanned the tiny cabin. There only a few things that seemed like her personal items scattered over the living area and the bathroom. The majority was in the bedroom. "I'll take here. You hit the other two?"

"Yes, ma'am." Leo gave a playful salute and then stepped into the living room, Watson right on his heels, casting me another accusatory glare over his shoulder before trotting out of view.

Sometimes Watson seemed unreasonably quick to be offended, but this time, I couldn't blame him. Knowing it was only a matter of time, and treats, I tried to decide where to begin. Not sure where to start or even what we were looking for, I went directly to the closet.

It seemed Alexandria and my uncle Percival were kindred spirits. She had more clothes than I would've taken on a two-week vacation, and all of them looked expensive and lush. Feeling a little silly, I patted them down, checking the pockets and feeling for any strange bulges within the material.

There was nothing. Next I moved to the drawers of the TV stand. Like the closet, they were full—undergarments, scarves, all sorts of various products and accessories. I didn't find anything there, either. I glanced at my cell; we'd been searching for almost ten minutes. "Any luck over there?"

"No. Nothing at all." As if they'd been waiting,

Leo and Watson stepped into the bedroom. "What have you done? Where would you like me—" He grinned down at Watson. "—*us* to help."

"You're already done with both rooms?"

He shrugged one shoulder. "There wasn't much."

"I've done the closet and TV stand. We've got suitcases, that desk over there, and the bed itself." I headed toward the stack of suitcases. With all their pockets and zippers, they looked like the most work. "I'll start in on these."

"Okay, I'll get going on the desk." Though not needed, Leo tapped his thigh, inviting Watson to follow him.

Alexandria had brought five suitcases. She might actually be outdoing Percival. What solitary person owned *five* suitcases? I was working through the third one when I realized why they were striking me as strange. "There is not a solitary piece of scrap paper, abandoned string of dental floss, gum wrappers, or loose change in any of these. It's like they're brand-new." I started to look up at Leo but paused to inspect the ribbing stitched on the outside of the suitcases. Sure enough. "But there's a significant amount of wear and tear on the suitcases themselves. Not like they've been abused, just well used and well traveled."

Leo paused from flipping through one of the books from the stack on the desk. "Maybe she's just really neat."

"There's not even lint, Leo." I ran my hand inside the bottom crease of one of the pockets, then held up my fingers as if for inspection. "Nothing."

He considered for a second. "So... you're thinking they're spotless because they were recently cleaned free of evidence, more than Alexandria is a neat freak?"

"Maybe..." I gestured toward the closet and the TV stand. "Although everything's hung up and put away tidily, like she moved in here. But... still..."

"You've got great instincts. If your gut is telling you something's fishy about the suitcases, I bet money that you're right." He turned back to flipping through the pages. "If Alexandria did kill Luca, she would've had enough time to come back here and get rid of any evidence that might be incriminating."

"Maybe so, but where? It isn't like she could drive it away." I scanned the room, paused when I glanced toward the living room. "The fireplace could help get rid of all kinds of things."

"True. There's also about a gazillion tons of snow

to cover up stuff for a while as well." Leo continued flipping as he responded, then set the book down, picked up another, and started flipping again. "As far as things that someone would be willing to kill for, it could be anything—weapons, drugs, cash, poached antlers, or..." He flinched, staring at whatever he'd found in the book, then went sheet white.

I stood. Likewise, Watson rose to attention, feeling the change in the air. "What did you find?"

Leo shook his head, closed the book, and looked toward me. "Nothing. I..." He blinked, then shook his head again, though this time it seemed in resignation rather than denial. "You're not gonna like it, and it won't be easy. But..." He crossed the room, met me in the middle, handed me the book, his thumb holding the page. "Here."

I took it like it was a ticking bomb, a sense of dread growing as I turned to the page. It looked to be a sketchbook. It seemed Alexandria Bell was a skilled artist. Remarkably skilled artist, judging from the instant recognition of the face staring up at me. Knees suddenly feeling weak, I sank to the bed, gaping at the page.

"He's younger." Unable to stop myself, I smoothed a fingertip over his face, smearing the drawing slightly. "They both are."

Leo sat beside me, and feeling my mood, Watson did as well, pressing his warm flank to my shins and resting one of his paws on the top of my foot. "You okay?"

I nodded slowly, then realized how it must look to Leo, so I refocused on him, meeting his eyes so he could see the truth of my words. "I *am* okay. Shocked as it was rather unexpected. But I am okay. There are no feelings or anything like that."

"Fred, it's okay if there are. It's only natural that—"

I cut him off with a shake of my head. "There aren't." My words sounded harsher than I'd meant them, but they weren't really directed toward Leo. "There aren't." I softened my tone before looking back at the drawing of a much younger Alexandria with a much younger Branson Wexler standing beside her, one arm draped over her shoulders, pulling her in close.

"Wow. You really are something." Alexandria glared at me, looked back down at the sketchbook I'd tossed in front of her, then sneered at Susan by my side. "Kiss your badge goodbye, honey. It'll be too bad that you're losing the shine, though. It's the only piece of jewelry that looks good on a mannish frame like yours."

"Come on. There's no reason to—"

Susan cast a glare of her own at Leo, cutting him off, before addressing Alexandria, her tone professional and cold. "Insults aren't going to help you, Ms. Bell. Some explanations are in order."

"I'll say." Alexandria repositioned the wooden armchair, fully at ease. "You practically dragged me from my cabin and—"

"No one dragged you, Ms. Bell."

Alexandria cocked an eyebrow. "You practically

dragged me from my cabin, and then proceed to allow it to be broken into by these two." She looked at me again. "And probably that mutt of yours. Not only will I have the cop's badge, but I'll sue you for every stray hair and stain on my property"—without a break she returned to Susan—"and to top it off, you're interrogating me without a warrant, right next to, judging from the bloodstains, where that boy was killed."

That had thrown me off as well when Leo and I had walked back into the main lodge, only to have Lisa tell us Susan had taken Alexandria to the library game room. I'd barely glanced to where Luca's body had been before I'd shown Susan what Leo and I had found.

"Don't forget to add this to your bevy of complaints." Susan picked up the key letter opener in an evidence bag she'd placed on a nearby table. Slight mocking entered Susan's voice when Alexandria merely rolled her eyes. "You're not even going to pretend to be disturbed by the sight of the murder weapon you used?"

"I'm hardly a fainting flower." Alexandria smiled. "So that's it, then, you're truly accusing me of murder?" She gestured toward the sketchpad. "Because of this? How in the world is an old drawing of me and an ex-boyfriend tied to some poor waiter or custodian, whatever he was, getting himself killed?"

I flinched, despite myself.

Alexandria noticed but didn't have time to say anything before Susan responded.

"Acting so nonchalant around murder doesn't exactly put any cards in your favor."

"Like I said, I'm not a fainting flower." Alexandria barely spared Susan a glance before studying me, her blue gaze dipping down to Watson, who hadn't left my side since finding the sketchbook. After a second, she blinked, then her gaze traveled up and down my body before she met my eyes. "I'm a little embarrassed that I've been so slow to catch on. In my defense, you are about as far from his type as I could imagine."

Leo stiffened and stepped closer.

Alexandria didn't miss a beat, though she didn't spare Leo a glance, a wicked smile growing as she addressed me. "But apparently *you* do have a type. Tall, dark, and handsome. Gotta say, I'm impressed, if not completely baffled. What's your secret? I don't think I've known any other frumpy, dog-hair-covered bookworms who have such good luck as you.

Although... two in a row, that suggests something more than luck."

My cheeks burned, but I refused to let her get the better of me. "So you admit you dated Branson?"

She sneered. "Why wouldn't I admit that? The man's gorgeous and charming." She tapped the drawing again. "Plus, the proof is right here. We dated for quite a while. Though, as you can tell by the drawing, it was some time ago."

"Then how did you know about Winifred?" There was a growl in Leo's voice that nearly reminded me of Watson.

That time, she did look at him. "Excuse me?"

"You just implied that you somehow knew about the... relationship between Branson and Fred. If the two of you dated so long ago, how would you even know about her?"

I noticed Susan give Leo an approving nod, but any hope to snag Alexandria failed. Her cocky, entitled attitude didn't falter.

"I said we *dated* some time ago. Not that I hadn't seen him." She looked back at me, the challenge in her eyes. "We saw each other at Christmas. Just because we're not dating doesn't mean we can't... *see* each other from time to time. I'm not so small that I can't admit it hurt to see him upset about another woman. You really did a number on him. But still, it was me he ran to."

"You saw Branson... at Christmas?" Not long after he left Estes Park.

"Jealous?" She cocked her chin and gestured with a flick of her wrist toward the bloodstain. "Is this how you get your revenge?"

The bark of laughter that sounded was so unlike me it took a second to realize I was the one who'd made the sound. "Not hardly. And if you're the one carrying around the drawing you did years ago of the two of you, I'd say that's answer enough about who's jealous." Something about her demeanor helped snap me back into place, get over the unexpected shock of it all. When I spoke again, I was pleased to discover my voice sounded normal, strong, calm, and direct. "It's just more proof. Clearly your association with Branson Wexler, or whatever his real name is — " I paused for a heartbeat, seeing if there was any reaction, but there wasn't. "—is current. You saw him at Christmas, then show up here a couple weeks later, engage in suspicious activity at the back of a van during a blizzard, and then the young man who you caught recording you is murdered. I don't believe in coincidences."

She shrugged, unflappable and unconcerned. "I

don't see how any association with Branson, past or present, would have anything to do with the murder. Especially the murder of a member of the service team at a hotel."

I tried again, partially to push, partially out of curiosity. "You called him Branson Wexler."

Her brows knitted. "Of course I did."

"If you dated him years ago, what did you call him back then?"

"Branson Wexler." Alexandria looked at me as if I was daft. "I'm not really sure where you're going with all of this."

"Branson Wexler was an alias, a fairly new one." Susan spoke up, sounding impatient. Knowing her, she'd had enough of Alexandria attempting to mark Branson as her territory. "As Winifred implied, if you knew him many years ago, you knew him under his real name, or another alias. What was it?"

Confusion flitted over Alexandria's features, and I couldn't get a read on whether it was genuine, or if she was just an exceptional actress. "I'm afraid you've had faulty information. Branson Wexler was most definitely not an alias. It was his real name. We dated long enough I would know. I saw his driver's license, credit cards"—she shrugged—"everything. He was and *is* Branson Wexler."

Susan squatted, propping her elbows on her knees to be at eye level with Alexandria. With her heavily muscled body, somehow she was even more intimidating, like a mountain lion ready to pounce. "You're only making this worse for yourself. We know that can't possibly be true. He admitted as much to Winifred in person. You sticking to this story only makes you look guiltier."

This time, Alexandria stared Susan in the eye, then her gaze traveled to Leo and stopped with me. "I'm afraid I have no idea what any of you are talking about."

Susan was right. Though Alexandria was unshakable, not revealing a solitary chink in her armor, it was only more proof. Not only had she known and dated Branson, but she worked with and was just as skilled at deception as he was, clearly. My heart sped up, pounding painfully in my chest in a way that had absolutely nothing to do with Sergeant Wexler. I lowered my voice to a whisper, just in case it started to shake. "What role do you play in the Irons family?" I wanted to go further, demand to know if she had anything to do with my father's murder.

"The Irons family?" The glint of humor in her eyes confirmed we were right. "Is that another of

Branson's so-called aliases? Branson Irons doesn't have a very good ring, does it?"

Susan shocked us all by lurching forward and grabbing Alexandria by the shoulder. For the first time, Alexandria's unflappable demeanor broke. She let out a yelp and gave a wince of pain.

Moving at an impressive speed, with her other hand, Susan reached for handcuffs and had Alexandria's wrist secured to the arm of the chair before she could protest further. I started to reach for Susan, thinking she was about to do more to Alexandria than handcuff her, judging from the pure hatred covering Susan's face, but I pulled back as Susan stood. "You want to lie to us about last night as well? Tell us that *wasn't* you Luca recorded by the van?"

Seemingly unable to get her composure back, Alexandria gave a jerk of her wrist, rattling the handcuffs, and fury laced her words. "Not only will I have your badge, I'll see you behind bars. This is assault, harassment. You have absolutely no jurisdiction or right to—"

"Save it!" Susan nearly shouted, her fists trembling at her sides.

Watson whimpered and moved so he stood in between my legs.

At Watson's sound, Susan glanced down,

and took a breath before looking back at Alexandria. "What were you doing at the van last night?"

"None of your business," Alexandria bit back, not a bit of her fury evaporating.

Susan tried again. "What was so important in that van that you were willing to kill over?"

"I didn't kill that snooping brat." Alexandria rattled the handcuff again. "But the second I'm out of this chair, you're a dead woman."

Susan laughed. "Trust me, promising threats is only going to—"

"Let's take a break." Leo proved his bravery by putting a hand on the back of Susan's shoulder. She snarled, but he left it there. "Come on. All of us. This won't go anywhere good."

When Susan looked like she was going to argue, I chimed in. "I think it's a good idea. We could all use a breather." I turned, tapping my thigh for Watson to follow, and I hoped Susan and Leo would do the same. I'd been on the receiving end of Susan's disdain multiple times, but I'd never seen hate like that from her. I wasn't entirely sure what she was capable of.

"Come on." Leo spoke from behind me, sounding like he was attempting to soothe. "She's handcuffed. She's not going anywhere. Let's regroup."

I paused in the doorway until I heard their footsteps, and then continued. I nearly stopped once I was inside the key room, but from what I could see through the French doors, no one occupied the sofas in front of the fireplace. That would be better.

"She is so clearly lying it's disgusting," Susan bickered at Leo as we crossed the room. He started to reply, but she kept going.

Watson and I were nearly to the sofas before I noticed the small group of women clustered around the other set. They'd been out of view, hidden by the other side of the wall.

"Of course she's part of the Irons family." Susan was still going as she and Leo entered the lobby. "Which means she's also part of the stain over my police department. Which makes this a lot bigger than a solitary murder. We might not have Wexler here to interrogate, but this is as close as we've got. I'm not missing my chance for—"

"Susan." I had called her name twice before she stopped talking, and I nodded toward the group of knitters.

She followed the gesture and closed her mouth. She continued heading toward Watson and me, then paused and whirled on the women. "How many of you are part of the Irons family? Is this whole knitting group nonsense, some sort of cover? If I go out to the vans right now, will I find a whole bunch of drugs under your spools of yarn?"

"Susan!" My bark was sharp enough Susan flinched, and while she looked like she was going to argue for a moment, she didn't. Turning on her heels, she strode the rest of the way to me, then plopped down on the far side of the sofa.

Four of the knitters were present, and all four of them stared, wide-eyed and slack-jawed. The oldest, Minnie, and the youngest, whose name I couldn't recall, weren't present.

"Sorry." Leo attempted a smile. "It's been a stressful couple of hours. For everyone."

"That's okay. We understand." Cordelia recovered the quickest, though she glanced at Susan, then looked at me. "You really believe Alexandria had something to do with that boy's murder?"

I started to nod, then hesitated. I knew that information shouldn't be shared, but none of it was going according to protocol. It was a complete mess. Not the least of which was that Alexandria was right. She would be able to have Susan's badge over this and would doubtless bring charges against Leo and me for breaking into her cabin. Might as well go for broke—who knew, maybe Susan was onto something. If these women were part of the cover for the Irons family, perhaps seeing how they reacted would give us some answers. "We do. Yes."

"Alexandria..." Betsy blinked repeatedly, then looked toward her friends. "A murderer?"

All four of the women's expressions were mirror images of one another, their shock never fading. Cordelia shook her head. "That's... unsettling." She glanced toward the French doors as if trying to peer back to Alexandria, but there was no way she could see anything from her angle. "If we can help... in any way, please say."

I expected Susan to go off again, demanding they confess to being part of the crime ring that had so disrupted our lives and our town. She didn't.

"Thank you." I considered questioning them but wasn't even sure where to begin. Even if I did, I would only increase the odds of another outburst. "For now, would you mind giving us a little privacy?"

"Of course. No problem at all." Cordelia nodded seriously, and as she stood, the other three followed suit.

"Thank you so much. We appreciate it." The other women—Cordelia's sister, Pamela, Wanda, and

Betsy nodded their agreement, though they still looked shell-shocked.

Cordelia gave a friendly nod toward Watson as they headed to the front door, but he stayed where he was.

Before I could sit, Katie and Anna passed the group of women on their way out of the dining room.

"You caught the murderer already, didn't you?" Anna hurried over, passing Katie, her hands fluttering. "I must say, Fred, this is record speed for you. It's only been a matter of hours." She bent toward Watson. "Of course you helped, didn't you, little angel?"

Watson slunk backward, staying out of reach of her hands.

"Poor dear." She straightened, looking partially offended. "He's clearly thrown off and beside himself."

I started to respond but noticed several other members of my family and the anniversary party heading our way from the dining room as well.

"Get back!" Susan's voice rose again, and she appeared beside me, pointing toward the dining room. "All of you. This is an official police investigation, and we don't need your intrusion."

"Well, I never!" Anna gasped in full blown

offense that time, her hand coming to rest on her bosom. "Of all the—"

"Oh, save it, Anna!" Susan gestured again, this time her pointed finger shaking. "Move it!"

Casting me a wide-eyed stare before coming to the rescue, Leo addressed the group. "Guys, sorry, things are a bit of a mess. You might give us a few minutes? We will fill you in when we can."

"No, we won't. It's none of your alls—"

"Susan!" Leo hissed at her, and she backed down, her cheeks growing redder. He turned back to the group once more. "If you don't mind."

There were a few murmurs of assent, and the group turned and headed back into the dining room, Anna practically sputtering as she left.

Before Katie turned to join them, I motioned her over.

Susan cast me a warning glare but didn't protest, surprisingly.

I took a couple of minutes and filled in Katie. Though she looked nearly as shocked as the group of knitters, she accepted it quickly and nodded. "You know, it doesn't mean much, but it's one more little puzzle piece, as you say." She held my gaze, as if treading lightly. "The knitting group is from Willow Lane, some little town in the Ozarks. That would be close to Kansas City, right? Where you grew up?"

Her gentle way of saying, *close to where your dad was killed*. I took a steadying breath and nodded. One more puzzle piece indeed. "Which means Alexandria lived close to the heart of the Irons family headquarters, at least from all we've figured out."

"That also means they could be involved. I'm tempted to arrest the whole lot of them." Susan's tone was quieter but just as brisk. "Although I only have one pair of handcuffs."

Leo petted Watson silently as I explained all the details to Katie. When he spoke, it sounded as if he was addressing himself as much as the rest of us. "Either way, whether we're just talking about Alexandria, all of them, or something in the middle, the bigger question is why are they here? Why now? That can't be a coincidence."

All three of us turned to look at him, and a cold dread settled in my gut. "You mean... they're meeting other members of the Irons family here."

"Here?" Katie looked around nervously. "As in Baldpate or Estes Park in general?"

He shrugged. "Either. Both."

From the other side, I stroked Watson as well, trying to push my fear away. The feeling was ridiculous. It wasn't like any of this was a surprise. "It makes sense. Branson said there were other members of the Irons family in Estes, even ones he didn't know about." I looked toward Susan. "Even Alexandria said as much, in her own way. When she was threatening your badge at the cabin. She said she had contacts here."

Susan's pale blue eyes widened, and she nodded. "You're right. Not exactly a confession, but... close." She looked around too, though not as nervously as Katie, nor like she was seeing spies everywhere. "From the research I've done, the Irons family also has ties internationally. Maybe one of the exchange kids is involved. Or..." She gave a little shake of her head, uncharacteristically looking embarrassed or something.

I finished the thought for her. "Or part of the anniversary celebration."

She nodded.

"No." Leo shook his head, looked over his shoulder into the dining room as if he could see everyone, then shook his head again. "No. None of us would do that."

"We would have said the same thing about Branson." Katie sounded heartbroken, as if it was a guarantee we had another betrayer in our midst.

"*I* wouldn't have," Susan snarled. "Maybe I didn't know exactly what it was, but I told everybody who would listen Branson was nothing more than a snake."

That was true, she had.

Several more minutes passed, each of us caught in our own mix of fear, suspicion, and worry. All except for Watson, who gave a happy grunt and twisted around so he could get a double-handed belly scratch from Leo and me.

He soothed me, just a bit. Enough to take the edge off so I could breathe a touch easier. I didn't want to consider that a member of my family or one of our friends could be involved in any of this. It was too much, and nothing that could be figured out at the moment. "Okay, that's out there now, and we'll have to deal with it at some point. But in this instance, let's focus on Alexandria."

Susan brightened, though her smile was dark. "Good point. But maybe you're wrong. She may hold the answers to all of it. She can point out the other snake among us."

She started to stand, but Leo reached out and grabbed her arm. "Don't act irrationally. We're already in deep water as it is."

"I'm not going to kill her or anything so ridiculous." Susan wrinkled her nose in disgust but stayed where she was. I couldn't help but marvel at the camaraderie she and Leo had. "But you make a good point. We're *already* in deep water, especially me. What's a bit more pushing going to hurt?"

To my surprise, Leo tilted his head as if acknowledging the idea. "Fine. But we don't hurt her. We don't become the bad guys in order to catch bad guys."

Katie and I exchanged glances, and as much as I wanted to disagree with Leo, I couldn't. "Okay, but before we go back in there, let's plan this thing out. What direction do we want to head? And we need some guidelines or rules. If—" I started to say Susan's name and barely caught myself. "If someone starts to get carried away or loses their temper to a dangerous degree, we all step in and stop it."

The next several minutes were lost in the debate of protocol and boundaries. To my relief, that part wasn't so hard. Then we started mapping out the plan, different angles to try to break Alexandria's reserve, coming up with questions and ways to ensnare.

Katie joined us as we walked back through the key room. As we approached the doorway, this time

Watson didn't growl. His full attention was focused on Leo as he happily trotted between the two of us.

Susan halted after she stepped in and then let out an angry curse.

Behind her, the rest of us froze.

Across the room, still handcuffed to the chair, Alexandria sat, her head lolled back, the old-fashioned key handle of the letter opener, still wrapped in the clear evidence bag, protruding from her heart.

THIRTEEN

"I don't think it's legal for you to be able to keep us all in here." Minnie, the oldest member of the knitting group, glared at Katie, Leo, and me from her spot at the dining room table, her gnarled hands never ceasing to wield the knitting needles. "We came out here on vacation, to knit, to enjoy the mountains, not to be held prisoner."

"We're not holding you prisoner, and we're only doing what the local law enforcement asked." I addressed Minnie, then scanned the room. "Officer Green simply wants everyone together in one place."

Minnie wasn't finished. "That woman officer isn't here right now. So you really don't have any authority to—"

"Leo is a park ranger," Katie spoke up, pointing across me to Leo. "He's a federal employee and can step in for law enforcement when needed."

I wasn't sure about the accuracy of that statement.

Leo's eyes bugged slightly, but before he could respond, Watson chose that moment to rear up on his hind legs and bump Leo's thighs with his forepaws, demanding attention.

"We're fine. We'll help in any way we can." Cordelia sat across the table from Minnie and sounded like she was reprimanding a child, though the woman was a couple decades older than herself. "Besides, everyone is trapped in here, thanks to the snow. We've got tons of wonderful food, we're warm, and we're safe."

"Safe? Really?" Minnie seemed nonplussed. "Did you forget about that poor boy who had his throat slit this morning? I'd hardly call that safe." She reached for a slice of the cornbread, took a bite, and then spoke with her mouth full while holding a half-finished sweater away from crumbs. "You're right about the food, though."

A couple of the other knitters shook their heads in embarrassment, and Cordelia sent me apologetic grimace.

At that moment, their youngest member, Cassidy, hurried in and joined them at her spot at the table. If I was counting correctly, she was the final person missing out of everyone, except for Susan.

The two sets of French doors that led from the dining room to the glassed-in front porch were open, revealing the blizzard continuing to blow outside, though it seemed less ferocious as the sun was able to break through. No one was seated on the porch, however. The members of my family and the anniversary party were gathered around multiple tables closest to the French doors, all of them looking strained and concerned, but not offering any resistance, of course.

The knitting group sat at their normal spot in the center. Alexandria's chair was the only empty seat, but by that point, everyone knew she'd been taken in for questioning, so no one asked where she was.

The Baldpate staff made up a few tables on the far side of the room. Some of them had also been slow to wander in. Lisa sat with an arm around Juliet, who had yet to stop crying. The only member missing was Beau, as he was with Susan.

Had it really only been the night before that the space had been filled with joy and revelry as we celebrated Percival and Gary? It was just as beautiful and cozy as then. If anything, more so with the lack of electricity. The room was lit from what filtered in through the windows and the countless candles and lanterns spread throughout the room. The wood in the old iron stove sitting in the middle of the room crackled and popped happily. Even so, it felt a little ominous, and a little claustrophobic, despite the massive size of the hotel. We were trapped, with a murderer. That feeling hadn't sunk in when we'd thought it was Alexandria—we'd had a name, and within a few moments, the woman herself. But now, there was another killer, at least one, within the walls of Baldpate Inn. The thought sent a shiver down my spine, which surprised me, considering all I'd seen over the past year or so. But this felt different somehow.

Once more I scanned the room, skimming over the members of my family and the anniversary party. Between the six remaining knitters, Lisa, and five remaining staff members, not counting Beau, that left too many possibilities for my liking. Though my gut instantly cut out both Lisa and Cordelia as possibilities. Even as the thought crossed my mind, I added them back in. With a sinking feeling, I glanced back at the tables filled with people I knew and loved, my mind filtering in Alexandria's "connections" and Branson's past confession that there were other members of the Irons family in Estes, even ones he didn't know about.

It was too awful to consider. No wonder this time felt different.

All eyes focused behind us, and at the sound of steps, Katie, Leo, and I all turned. Beau walked in, his expression like he'd been put through an emotional wringer. Susan followed not far behind. As Beau joined the staff, Susan stood beside Leo, casting a scowl down at Watson when he gave a little territorial growl for being too close to one of his idols.

Her expression didn't change as she looked up at the room, but she hesitated, just for a second. It was the first time I'd seen her uncertain—even when her own brother had been accused of murder, she'd been decisive. But the moment passed quickly, and she lifted her chin and raised her voice. "Alexandria Bell was killed about an hour ago."

The room went dead still for half a second and then chaos erupted. Anna let out a scream. One of the knitters, Pamela, I thought, did as well, though it didn't reach the volume or shrillness of Anna's. Angus stood, his face ghost-white and anger flaring in his eyes. Beside him Gerald flinched, knocking over a bottle of his kombucha, splashing it over Percival and my mom. Percival let out a screech as well, at that. The only table that didn't react in panic was the staff. Lisa covered her mouth, her eyes wide with horror. Her cluster of young employees looked startled, and, as one, turned toward Lisa as if she were their mother hen.

"That's it! I'm not staying here another minute." Minnie stood, lifting one of the knitting needles as if brandishing a sword and shooting a glare over the room. "Whichever one of you is going on a killing spree, just try me. I won't hesitate to shove this through your eye!"

Cordelia reached out, trying to calm her, but Minnie shook her off.

"Everyone, just hold—" Leo moved forward, raising his voice, but Susan shot out a hand, jerking him back.

She didn't even bother to glare at Watson when he growled threateningly.

One glance at her revealed what Susan was doing, her pale blue eyes shrewd as her gaze darted from person to person, table to table. I didn't know if it was the best plan as far as keeping order, but I had to admire her daring. Drop a bomb and observe the reactions.

"I'm with the old one!" Anna stood, pointing toward Minnie, then turned to Barry. "Can you drive us out of here on that snowmobile you used this morning?"

"Anna Hanson, get a grip!" Susan barked at her for the second time, seeming almost more annoyed that Anna had distracted her observation than for the outburst itself. "No one's going anywhere, even if it was a possibility."

"You can't keep us here!" Minnie shook her knitting needle again. "We're all in danger!"

"Yes. I can." Susan took a couple of steps forward and placed a hand on the grip of her holstered gun. Though her words had been firm and clear, she now raised her voice to a near shout. "Everyone sit down and shut up!"

They did. Anna plopped down instantly, looking offended. Minnie seemed to be judging her chances, and then she, too, sat, after another tug from Cordelia.

Once more, Susan studied the room, slowly, methodically, her hand never leaving her holster. It seemed she met every single gaze in the place. She wasn't handling things the way I would, but I couldn't help but be impressed with her control, her power. Finally, Susan's stance relaxed, but the authority in her tone didn't. "There have been two deaths in the past twelve hours. From what we could tell, we apprehended the first killer, but as she was also murdered, we clearly have another killer."

Still her eyes tracked the room, and I found myself following her example, watching the expressions flicker and change over people's faces. Noticed the kombucha bottle tremble in Gerald's hands as he chugged what remained. The looks of fear that Zelda and Verona exchanged before they turned their gazes to their children. The expression of nausea that rose over Pamela's face. The glare of defiance and hate Beau shot in Susan's direction.

Finally she spoke again. "Considering we're snowed in during a blizzard, that means someone in this room... maybe multiple someones in this room... is a murderer."

At that, people's gazes left Susan and the rest of us in the front of the room and turned on one another. Expressions altering from disbelief, to fear, to suspicion.

Once more Susan waited, once more I observed. And what I saw was telling. The knitters were the only group where not a single set of eyes looked at another member—every one of the women, whether in fear or suspicion looked toward the strangers around them. But there were those of the staff whose gazes flicked to someone sitting at their table, lingering a moment as if wondering, *Is it you?* My heart hurt when I noticed the same thing at the tables occupied by my family and friends. Noah turned narrowed eyes on Carl. Barry's gaze flicked to Angus. Even my own mother cast a suspicious glance toward Gerald, then, as if feeling me studying her, looked at me, a sad expression in her eyes.

Susan let the final ball drop. "Furthermore, one, or more of you, we believe, is involved with the crime ring known as the Irons family."

That time I kept my attention fully focused on the ones I knew best, praying and hoping I didn't see confirmation of my worst fears. Without exception, every single member of the anniversary party flinched—everyone, even Ocean and Britney, the oldest of my nephews and nieces. Nearly every resident of Estes Park knew of the Irons family by that point—for a couple of weeks after Branson left, the *Chipmunk Chronicles* ran a series of articles about the organization. Considering both the town's police chief and sergeant were members, that only made sense. Maybe I'd wasted the opportunity to discover some telltale reaction from someone at the other tables.

Without fail, every member of my group looked shocked as well. And that also made sense. Even though they all knew about the Irons family, like me, they hadn't expected it to show up here. Although... could some of those shocked expressions only be caused by Susan and the rest of us discovering that connection? Maybe... I couldn't tell.

When I met Mom's gaze, I recognized my own fear and hurt. It was almost more than I could take, knowing those remotely responsible for my father's death were near. I could only imagine how that knowledge cut through her.

What little murmuring had occurred died down. Susan spoke again, this time addressing the table of knitters. "Why are you all here again?"

The question surprised me, both that she began there and that she'd ask it in front of the whole group instead of splitting everyone up.

Minnie scowled, but the rest of the women all looked toward Cordelia. I wasn't sure if she was the leader of the knitting group or not, but clearly they all deferred to her.

If she was offended, she didn't let on, her voice calm and clear as she spoke to Susan. "We have a knitting club back home. My sister"—she motioned to Pamela—"found out that Alexandria was planning another trip to Estes Park. She'd heard about the Cozy Corgi bakery and wanted to visit. She—"

"What in the world does a knitting club have to do with baking?" Susan interrupted and cast an accusatory glance toward Katie.

Cordelia opened her mouth to respond, but Pamela beat her to it, sounding flustered. "That's why *I* wanted to come. Alexandria had talked a lot about the Knit Witt shop and how skilled Mr. Witt was... er... is. So I thought it would be a good excuse. Plus, some of us needed a..." Her eyes widened and her words trailed off, as she cast an apologetic glance at another one of the members.

"Needed a what?" Susan's impatient tone was almost soothing in its constancy.

"Needed a break, needed to get away." The only black woman of the group, Wanda, I believed, spoke up, her voice resigned. "My father passed away during the holidays. It's been an exhausting couple of months."

Pamela spoke up again, rushing forward as if she was trying to rescue Wanda. "It really is all my fault. Inasmuch as I don't want to admit it, I guess I did invite us along on Alexandria's trip. She wasn't overly happy about it, but..." Her cheeks pinked. "I suppose it's bad to speak ill of the dead, but Alexandria was irritated and short a lot of the time. So it didn't seem like anything unusual."

"The knitting club is not a cover for something else." Cordelia spoke up again, addressing Susan with a level stare. "The three of us"—she motioned at Wanda and Pamela—"also have a food delivery business, but that's the only other organization attached in any fashion to our knitting club. This was merely a vacation, a chance to grow as friends." She glanced across the room toward Angus. "And hopefully grow in our skills by meeting with a master knitter."

Susan studied the group for a second. "Any of you want to confess to nighttime wanderings last night?"

Confusion flitted over their faces as the women looked at one another, but I noticed Cassidy glanced down at the table, her cheeks pinking like Pamela's had moments before.

"Interesting." Susan surprisingly didn't push. She turned toward the anniversary party. "Angus, from the rumor mill, I gather you had an ongoing sexual relationship with the deceased?"

He flinched and anger flashed in his eyes. "Please show some respect, Officer Green. Both for Alexandria and myself."

Susan rolled her eyes. "Fine. A *romantic* relationship. Is that better?"

Gerald shifted uncomfortably, casting a commis-erating glance at his friend.

Angus bristled. "Not much, no. And I'll not be discussing such private matters in this setting. I will answer any questions you want to give in a more respectable manner and in private. Until then, I will say that, like many of us in town, I've known Alexandria for years. She was an exceptional artist, demanding, and a creative soul. I also knew that she and the knitting group were coming, though they were earlier than expected. I had plans to do a knitting demonstration with them the day after tomorrow. Once we were all back in town."

Susan looked like she was going to press the point, but then switched tactics. "What about the rest of you? Any nighttime adventures any of you need to get off your chests?"

And again, those suspicious gazes flitted about my family and friends, causing an ache.

For a second, I wondered where Susan was going with that questioning, then remembered she'd met with Beau on her own. I was willing to bet she'd gotten the password for Luca's cell phone once more. Goodness knows what he'd managed to capture in his spying, or documenting, as he would've described it. The thought caused me to give a flinch of my own, and I glanced at Susan. Had Luca captured the moment between Leo and me?

"No volunteers on that one either, I see." Susan shook her head in disgust and turned toward the staff table. "Which one of you is Darrell?"

A handsome redheaded man, who appeared slightly older than the rest of the staff, maybe twenty-two or twenty-three, raised a hand and looked terrified.

Susan narrowed in on him with a laser-focused stare. "Where are you from, Darrell?"

He swallowed. "Uhm. Eureka Springs."

"Arkansas, correct?"

He nodded.

"And Arkansas is in the Ozarks, correct?"

He nodded again.

Susan turned her attention toward the knitters. "And Willow Lane is in the Ozarks as well?"

Cordelia and a couple of the others nodded.

Susan turned to our group, focusing on my mother. "As is Kansas City, right?"

Mom shook her head. "Technically—"

"Is it close, Phyllis?" Susan snapped at my mom, reminding me that though things had improved between the Green family and my own, there was a long history of hard feelings.

"Comparatively, yes." Mom started to nod and froze, things clicking into place. She cast wide eyes on me, then turned in her seat, looking first at the knitting group, then to Darrell. After a second she looked back at me, her gaze knowing.

I glanced at Susan as I tried to catch my breath. She'd connected those dots quickly. Surely that was too much coincidence. The Irons family being centered from Kansas City, where my father had been killed. A knitting group from the nearby Ozarks with a newly deceased member with direct ties to the Irons family. And an employee of the inn also from the Ozarks, when all the rest of the staff were international.

Susan tried once more. "I'll ask one more time. Anyone want to come clean about their nighttime activities? There're only two people I trust in this room at the moment..." She glanced toward Leo and me, which in and of itself was startling, then her gaze settled on Katie, and her nose wrinkled in dislike. "Well... three of you, I suppose." She turned back to the group. "As far as I'm concerned, every single one of the rest of you is a suspect. Speaking up now might go a long way."

The room stayed silent.

I exchanged glances with Leo. I could tell he was

also wondering if we were subjects of Susan's viewing.

"Fine, then," Susan spat. "We're done. You're all to stay in this room." Once more she looked at Katie. "Are you capable of keeping watch? From everything I've seen from you, you're the biggest teacher's pet there is. Surely you can tattle if someone tries to leave." She didn't give Katie a chance to answer before looking back at everyone. "It's going to be a long afternoon of questioning, so sit tight. And for all that's holy, please refrain from killing anyone else."

Lisa sucked in a quick gasp from across the room, drawing everyone's attention to her. She flinched before pointing toward the wall of windows. "The snow has stopped."

Again the entire room turned as one toward the opposite side. Sure enough, somewhere in the group interrogation, the blizzard had ceased. The sky was bright blue and filled with gray fluffy clouds. The sight was stunningly gorgeous. Under a few feet of snow, the world outside looked like the landscape of another planet. In the middle of it all, barely visible, lay Estes Park, glittering in a way that hid all the chaos Susan reported was going on in town. Which was fine; we had enough chaos of our own to deal with.

Susan clapped her hands, pulling all attention back to her. "While that's good news, it doesn't change anything. Even if the blizzard doesn't start again, we have no idea how long it will take for electricity to return, and for us to get any help up here. Until then, I'm in charge, and we're going to catch ourselves a murderer."

Angus sat on the opposite couch and bent slightly so he could lower his hand close to the floor. Watson left his spot between Leo's and my feet, crossed the short distance, and sniffed the offered palm. "Such a good, handsome little man." Genuine affection filled Angus's warm voice.

Watson gave the hand a lick, then nudged demandingly with his nose.

Following directives, Angus scratched Watson's head, eliciting a cloud of dog hair. A hint of a smile played on his lips before he laughed softly. "He is his own little blizzard, isn't he?"

"It's true." I studied the interaction between the two of them, trying to decide if I could read into Watson's behavior. "Thanks to corgis, the lint roller companies will never be in danger of going out of business."

Angus laughed again, though the humor didn't reach his eyes. "I did have to do a thorough vacuuming of the yarn shop after Watson's visit. Even so, a couple days later there were occasional fur balls floating across the hardwood floor."

"Are you two kidding me with this?" Susan sounded thoroughly disgusted and shot a glare between Angus and me. "If that dog is going to be a distraction, shut him outside. You just proved he has enough fur for him to be warm and toasty."

Before I could give in to my temper and say something I probably wouldn't regret, Leo patted his knee. In response, Watson whirled and rushed back, smashing into Leo's shins, and looking utterly pleased at the impact.

"You're a good police officer, Officer Green. Intelligent and canny." Angus straightened and settled back into the sofa. "You'll be a *great* one when you learn that you catch more flies with honey."

"Save it, Angus. I'm hardly taking career advice from an old man who spends his days knitting and his nights wasting time on role-playing games with my brother." Susan shot me a warning glare from the other side of our couch but didn't make any more threats toward Watson.

We'd moved two of the sofas from the lobby into

the key room, the French doors giving more privacy, but allowing us to be close enough to the dining room that if there was a revolt, we could hear. There'd been no debate about who to speak to first, not that Susan had given Leo or me a chance for input. As soon as we'd set the couches a few feet apart, facing each other in some sort of cozy interrogation-room resemblance, Susan demanded Angus join us.

"Interesting that your girlfriend was just murdered a hot second ago and you're in here laughing and playing with an overstuffed puppy." Susan refocused on Angus, leaning forward so her elbows rested on her knees, her muscular shoulders flexing beneath the fabric of her uniform. "Was there a recent lovers' spat?"

His green eyes flashed in anger, as they had before in the dining room. It was an unusual expression on Angus.

"Oh, sorry." Susan didn't sound sorry in the slightest. "That not have enough honey for you? Well then, you're really not going to like my next inquiry. How much older are you than Alexandria? Twenty, twenty-five years? I'm wondering if she decided to trade you in for someone younger? Maybe someone *much* younger."

I spared a quick glance at Susan and noticed Leo doing the same thing. She sounded like she had a theory, a specific one.

Angus's lips thinned, but when I decided he wasn't going to answer, he spoke, his voice tight and hard. "Alexandria was free to do as she wished. As was I."

Susan scoffed. "Really? You expect me to believe that? You're a little old for one of those newfangled open relationships, aren't you?"

Anger flashed once more, then faded to something else, something removed and distant as Angus shook his head. "I'm sorry you're so miserable, Susan. Life doesn't have to be this way." Her hands clenched, but he kept going. "Regardless, despite what you think you may know, we were not in a relationship. Alexandria was not my girlfriend."

When Susan didn't reply instantly, I looked over. She was nearly shaking in rage. It seemed Angus's arrow had struck its mark.

Leo jumped in, his tone softer. "Sorry to pry into your personal affairs, Angus, but from what I gathered, the gossip seems to be that you and Alexandria had more than a friendship. I think that's clouding the issue at the moment."

"We did have more than friendship. We were

two consenting adults." His green eyes shot a challenge at Susan. "Even if I was a couple decades her senior, as you've so delicately pointed out. But it was one of... convenience and respect, nothing more."

I liked Angus, from what little I knew. His yarn shop was one of the most beautiful stores in town, and his talent was awe-inspiring. Not to mention, while Watson didn't go bonkers with love over him, he clearly felt safe with the man, and that went a long way. At the same time, I couldn't disagree with Susan—something about his reaction was off. "Maybe it's my Midwest sensibilities, but you do seem rather... calm and collected about Alexandria's murder, considering you two were involved, even if in a nontraditional way."

He smiled and held out his hand to me as he addressed Susan. "You should take lessons. There wasn't even honey involved, yet I don't feel like I'm being taunted by a child." Then he focused on me. "I'm not one for hysterics, but no, even if I was, I don't think this would be a situation that would cut me as deeply as people would assume it should." He folded his hands in his lap, and for the first time his gaze drifted away, as if reliving a memory. "Alexandria wasn't a kind woman; she wasn't mean, either. In a lot of ways, she was distant and cold. However,

she was intelligent, ardent, and insanely talented."
Warmth crept into his smile then. "I think that's the
biggest loss. Within a couple of years, her knitting
skills would've surpassed mine. Who knows what
she would've accomplished? I respected her,
admired her, and we had a few deep and strong
bonds. Outside of that, we were very different
people. There were things about her I didn't like. She
would've said the same about me." Another glance
toward Susan. "There were times she found me just
as insufferable as you're feeling about me right now,
I'd wager. I'm sorry she's dead. I will miss her, but
I'm not heartbroken. If anything, I'm angry. About
how she was killed. And... how, it seems, I was
deceived."

"Deceived?" Susan spoke again, finally. "Deceit
and betrayal are excellent motives."

"Yes, I suppose they are." Angus sounded unconcerned. "If what you're saying is true, a woman I've
known for years, one I've had a relationship with, not
only killed the young man in the night, but was
involved with an organization that's touched all of
our lives recently."

"*If* what I'm saying is true?" Susan bit out the
words. "Do you have a reason to believe I'm wrong?"

He nodded toward me. "I've become an admirer

of Miss Page, of her intelligence, deductive reasoning, and tenacity. But this is quick, even for her. I can't imagine what evidence any of you have found that would link Alexandria to the Irons family. If it's such an extensive crime organization as we've been led to believe, that would be a massive slipup. It would seem to me, in our desperation to understand and tie things with the pretty little red bow, we've jumped to conclusions."

As he spoke, though I wasn't sure why, it was like I saw a ribbon weaving its way through the picture, indeed tying itself into a pretty little red bow. Alexandria's connection to the Irons family, the knitting group, to Kansas City, to Angus's yarn shop, all combusting at our time at the inn. It was too much coincidence, way too much. And Angus was a touch too controlled, almost... too perfect. Even as the puzzle pieces tried to fall together, I attempted to scatter them again. I liked the man, quite a lot. He was a lifelong friend of my stepfather. Every instinct I had said I could trust him, well, nearly every instinct. But hadn't that been true about Branson?

As if reading my mind, Susan took the sketchbook from where she'd laid it beside the couch, opened it to the saved page, and shoved it toward Angus. "Care to explain that?"

For the first time, Angus's composure slipped a bit, confusion crossing his expression as he stared at the drawing of the younger Alexandria and Branson in disbelief. "Where did you find this?"

"It was in her cabin, Angus." Still petting Watson with one hand, Leo leaned forward, and though there was respect and concern in his tone, I thought I caught something else, something that hinted he was thinking along the same lines as me. "It's hers. There's no doubt about it."

"No, there isn't." Angus didn't look up at Leo, keeping his focus on the drawing. "This is Alexandria's work. I'd know it anywhere. Like I said, she was talented. Even more so with a pair of knitting needles, which should tell you something." He studied it a bit longer and closed the sketchbook reverently, placing one hand on the cover, then looked at me. "Are you okay?"

There was such gentleness in his tone that it caught me off guard and somehow issued a quick stab of pain. I felt my lips move, but I couldn't make any words come out.

Angus shot Susan a glare, as if it was all her fault, then returned to me. "I can't help but feel somewhat responsible. From what I understand, in some ways you were closer to Sergeant Wexler than I was to

Alexandria, and other ways, less so, but I think his betrayal probably hurt you more than Alexandria's does me. I'm so sorry they're connected. I'm sorry you have to face it again."

Angus had told me before that if I ever needed anything, I only needed to come to him. At the memory, the sincerity in his offer, I felt the tug of guilt over my thoughts about him only moments before.

"I take it your doubt has been cleared?"

Angus ignored her for a few moments, keeping a sympathetic gaze on me, then finally handed the sketchbook back to Susan with a sigh. "Yes. I don't see any other way to interpret that. Over all the years we've known each other, I had no clue about her connection to Sergeant Wexler. Clearly, he wasn't the only one with the double life." With that, he straightened again, and the walls returned, both in his eyes and in his tone. "I'll answer any more questions you want, but let me take care of a few for you right off. I didn't kill Alexandria. Or that boy. I didn't know she was involved with the Irons family, but yes, I do believe you that she was. And while I do not agree with your methods or your attitude, Officer Green, in this case, perhaps they are justified. Obviously we have a killer among us."

"I'm not asking for your approval, Angus. I only want answers." Though the anger left Susan's voice, she was clearly unimpressed.

"Like I said, I'll answer anything you want. Furthermore, I'll help in any way you deem appropriate. Estes Park is my town, its residents are my friends, my family. I'll help cut out the infection that's threatening to spread its darkness. Just let me know what to do and I'll do it."

True to his word, Angus answered the rest of Susan's questions without hesitation. She peppered them so fast that it was nearly hard to keep track. *Where were you at the time of Luca's murder? Where were you at the time of Alexandria's murder? Did you wander around in the middle of the night? Did you meet Alexandria at the van?* On and on and on. For each question, Angus had a quick, simple, clear answer. At the end, before he patted Watson good-bye, he requested that we keep the specific details of his relationship, as he called it, or his arrangement as Susan called it, with Alexandria private, but said that if for some reason it would help bring light to the dangerous connections, that he would understand.

"I detest that man." Susan slammed the French door as she returned from accompanying Angus back to Katie's supervision in the dining room. "He acts so intelligent, superior, and informed, though he's done nothing but play along in my brother's childish negative behavior over the years."

Susan's older brother, Mark, was a challenging personality, much like Susan herself, and I couldn't blame her for her strained relationship with him. He wasn't a bad guy, necessarily, but selfish and short-sighted. However, Susan was fiercely loyal to him, and so anyone who aided in his irresponsibility was nearly as guilty as Mark himself.

"But if you put that aside, do you believe him about Alexandria?" I asked.

She scowled at my question but didn't answer as she crossed the room and plopped down into the spot Angus had occupied opposite us. Then she surprised me. "Honestly, I don't think I can put it aside. Which means I can't be unbiased on the situation. What do you two think?"

It seemed Leo was more accustomed to that sort of response from Susan than me as he responded instantly. "I'm not sure. I've always liked Angus. He's an extremely respected and valued member of the community. But..." He looked toward the sketch-book, then cast me an apologetic look before continuing. "It seems like a lot of coincidences piling up right now. A lot."

"That's where I'm falling, too." Maybe it was hypocritical for me to doubt him when I'd fallen for Branson's lies, but could Alexandria really have deceived him? Alexandria *and* Branson? I turned to Susan. "Did Branson and Angus have a relationship that you know of?"

"Like I've told you a billion times, I was not that scumbag's keeper." She frowned, sounding irritated again. "You'd know more than me. For all I know, the two of you might've gone on a double date with Alexandria and Angus."

I could feel Leo tense beside me, ready to come to my defense, but I cut him off. "We didn't, as much as I'm sure that disappoints you, and unless I'm forgetting something, I don't recall Branson ever mentioning Angus." I switched tactics, both to avoid more conflict with Susan and to simply give my brain a break from the constant reminder of betrayal. "You seemed to have another theory besides the Irons family when you were questioning Angus. More like you suspected Alexandria was having an affair."

She shrugged. "I did, though if Angus's explanation of the relationship is to be believed, it doesn't really matter. And there's no reason to really doubt that part of the story."

"Maybe so, but at this point, we can't sweep

aside anything." Watson had crawled onto the couch between Leo and me when Angus left. I stroked him absently as my gaze flitted around the key room, taking in the thousands of keys and their individual labels lining the ceilings above our heads—so many stories, each one representing a different person, a different life. Probably each one with their own secrets, maybe even some had their own double lives. "Who did you think she was having an affair with?"

"That redheaded kid... man... whatever. Darrell." She said it with a sigh. "The one from the Ozarks. Again, one more coincidence. I almost pulled him in first, but Angus seemed so angry when we were speaking to the group that I decided we should start with him."

That had been my first inclination as well, but I'd forgotten about the redhead as we'd spoken to Angus. "But why did you think the two of them were having an affair? Because of where they lived?"

"No. Luca's phone." Susan shuddered. "That little guy was a creep. There's well over a hundred videos on there of him spying on people. I watched them until the battery died."

"I have an external charger. If you need it."

Susan waved Leo's offer away. "No. I'd finished the ones he'd shot from last night. The rest were of other members of the staff here. Last night"—she leveled a knowing stare at Leo and me, making me think Luca had caught our time in front of the fire —"was pretty much Grand Central Station here. It seemed like everyone was out of bed and roaming around. There were ones of Carl and Gerald—inasmuch as I said I don't trust anyone earlier, and that's true, I can no more see Carl or Gerald having the gumption to murder someone than my brother growing up enough to quit dressing up like an overgrown wizard. There was an interesting one of that old knitter woman, whatever her name is. But despite her attitude in there, what Luca caught wasn't sinister. It just looks like the old bat has a covert drinking problem. The one of the redhead—"

"Darrell." I spoke his name without a second thought.

"Like I care." She waved me off as well. "There was nothing incriminating about it either, except the way he moved. It was clear he was trying not to get caught; he was up to something."

"You suspect he might've been wandering off for a romantic interlude with Alexandria?" Leo's tone suggested he was pondering the idea, but then he shook his head. "Or meeting with her at the van."

Susan nodded.

Maybe so. Perhaps he was her touch point in Estes Park, both being centrally located to the heart of the Irons family organization. They might've made a trade or an exchange or a drop off at the van. Either way, though I hadn't seen the recordings, Darrell definitely looked nervous about something. Maybe he was the other figure in the blurry video. Perhaps he helped Alexandria kill Luca, then decided he'd better turn on Alexandria before she turned on him. Another thought hit me, and I looked back to Susan. "The vans. Do you think you can get the knitters to open them, or do we need to do another break and enter?"

Watson proved to be unpredictable yet again as the small herd of us made our way to the vans. He frolicked like a puppy in the path made by those ahead of us, bouncing along happily, leaping ungracefully in the air, attempting to catch snowflakes carried in the breeze, only to shove his face into the wall of snow with a chuff, pull back out with a sneeze, and start all over again.

When he stumbled in one of his leaps and bumped into the back of Cordelia's legs, she turned around to smile at him. "You're one of the happiest dogs I've ever seen." She paused to scratch the top of his head with her gloved hands and looked up at me. "I've met a couple other corgis during my day. I must say, Watson's the most cheerful one. The others seem to be rather grumpy and stubborn, though I found that quality endearing as well."

"Oh, trust me, you're seeing Watson on a good day, or a good moment. He's typically so grumpy he reminds me of those two cantankerous old man Muppets that complain about everything from their theater box seats. And he's almost as stubborn as I am."

Watson paused in his frolic to glare at me over his shoulder in apparent reprimand, then returned to his fun, lunged forward and dumped his head again in the wall of snow bordering our path.

"I think he was getting a little cooped up inside, so he's feeling extra playful. Not to mention that he's got two of his favorite people here, my stepfather and Leo." I motioned toward the front of our little parade, where Leo was clearing a path to the vans.

"I'm glad he's here. With the... events that are going on, it's nice to have some innocence." Cordelia looked like she was about to say more but instead smiled sadly at Watson, then turned to catch up with the rest of the group.

Though we expected a protest, the knitters had been instantly accommodating when Susan asked to see inside the vans. Four of them even joined Susan, Leo, and me. Only Cassidy and Minnie stayed back. The younger one still seemed distraught, and the older didn't want to risk walking in the deep snow.

Though the vans were parked less than a hundred yards from the inn, with the depth of the snow, it was slow going. I couldn't help but feel a little like prancing myself. I wasn't exactly tempted to shove my face in the snow, but it was good to be outside. The calm after the storm was remarkably beautiful—here and there, the weight of snow would be too much for an upper branch of a tree and cascade down in tumbling avalanches, like sparkling waterfalls over a cliff.

I used the time to shift through the small amount of information we had. Luca's death made sense. Horrible and a waste, but he'd caught Alexandria in an incriminating moment. And if she was part of the same group as Branson, I'd seen firsthand how nonchalant killing another person could be. I couldn't quite envision how the murder went down, but was close. Luca, startled at being caught, fleeing from the window while Alexandria sprinted over the parking lot and up the front steps. I wasn't sure if Luca had hidden his cell phone in the key room so he could claim he didn't know what she was talking about, or if he'd stumbled and it had slid. Maybe it didn't matter, but I was certain whatever had happened did so before Alexandria found him. From the way he was killed, I was willing to bet she'd expected to find it on his body, stuffed in a pocket or something. A quick slice of his throat didn't imply taking time to try to pry information out of him.

Had she looked for the cell phone? It hadn't appeared like it, nothing else was disturbed. Though from all the people that were up and about in the middle of the night, perhaps she heard someone walking about and fled. Either way, the second Luca had turned his cell phone on the scene at the van, he'd signed his death warrant.

But why Alexandria? My first inclination suggested it was the mystery person with her at the van. Eliminating another witness. But something about that didn't feel right either. If they were both members of the Irons family, wasn't there more strength in numbers? If anything, killing her only drew more attention to the coincidences, to the connections of Estes Park, Kansas City, the Ozarks. To Angus, to Darrell, possibly.

I hadn't reached any conclusions, not even close, when we finally arrived at the vans. Susan, Wanda, Betsy, and Pamela took the nearest, the one in Luca's recording. Leo, Cordelia, and I took the other.

Leo and I both let out matching sounds of awe as we opened the back doors of the van. Beside us, Cordelia chuckled. "It's a little type A, isn't it?"

Type A didn't begin to cover it. I'd never seen a vehicle packed so neatly. In fact, it reminded me a little of Angus's shop. Semitransparent plastic containers with pink drawer pulls lined the space, skeins of wool, arranged in descending gradient colors showing through. Each container had its own label—not the handwritten kind but the sort that had been done with a professional label maker.

"Yarn from sheep's wool has white labels, alpaca is yellow, angora goats are green, angora rabbits are purple." Cordelia pointed to one side of the van, then moved on to the other. "Over here we have patterns, knitting needles, crochet hooks... well, I guess you can read." She chuckled again.

"You were planning on getting some serious knitting done during this vacation." Leo reached for one of the container drawers and hesitated. "I'm almost afraid I'm going to mess up all your hard work."

"Oh no!" Cordelia shuddered. "That's not my handiwork. That's *all* Wanda. A place for everything and everything in its place. That's her motto. And don't worry about messing it up. Getting to the bottom of this is much more important than keeping the different hues of yarn together. Plus, I think she finds it soothing to rearrange. You'd give her a good excuse to get lost in her methods of madness."

"No wonder you brought two vans. I thought it was because there were seven of you, but it's because you brought a few stores' worth of materials along." I debated where to start. "Does the other van have this much? How long were you planning on staying?"

"This one was a supply van. Pamela, Wanda, and I took turns driving." She gestured toward the other, where Susan was bossing the other women around. "That was our luggage van. Alexandria drove it."

I started to reach for a drawer of knitting needles, though unsure why I'd chosen it, but studied Cordelia. "As in, she's the only one who drove it?"

Cordelia nodded, communicating with a cocked eyebrow rather than words.

"Control issues?"

"To say the least." Cordelia gestured toward the beautiful array of knitting supplies once more. "The same is true for Wanda, clearly. But... manifested in a very different way, and demeanor, for that matter."

Once more I started to turn back to the drawer, but there was a whimper and a jab against my calf. I looked down to find Watson glaring up at me, lifting one of his paws as if he was suddenly too dainty to have it touch the white fluffy stuff. "I tried to get you to stay at the inn. I told you you'd be warmer by the fire."

He whimpered again.

I glanced back the way we'd come, hating to lose the time, but maybe Watson wasn't just being his persnickety self. His paws were probably genuinely getting cold.

Before I could decide what to do, Cordelia bent, swept him into her arms, lifted with a grunt, and placed him in one sure motion in the back of the van, speedily enough she didn't even give Watson a chance to squirm or protest.

He stood there, surrounded by the knitting supplies, looking perplexed on how his world had suddenly shifted.

Leo laughed and ruffled his fur, spreading a cloud of dog fur and melting snow.

"Goodness. He is heavier than he looks." Cordelia rubbed the small of her back. "And that's saying something."

I marveled at her. "You're tougher than *you* look."

She waved me off with her free hand. "Sixty-five years of living on a farm tends to do a body good. I've lifted more than one calf to the back of a truck in my day. I wouldn't dare try that now. Luckily, little Watson here's not quite as heavy as a calf, but close."

I hoped I'd be as spry as Cordelia when I was her age.

With Watson satisfied, we got to work, going through drawer after drawer and finding nothing of interest or out of place. Not even anything mislabeled. We were probably wasting our time. Since Alexandria had driven the other van, the one that was in the recording, if there was anything to be found, it would be there. Even so, we kept going. After a few minutes, we decided to spread out. Leo continued with the supplies, Cordelia moved to the middle, searching the crevices of the seats, under mats, and pockets, and I took the front, rifling through the contents of the glove compartment. Watson stayed with Leo.

"What's this thing?" After a minute or two, Leo held up a large purple plastic tool that resembled a mangled umbrella missing the fabric.

Cordelia and I both peered toward the back from our respective places.

"Oh! I actually know that one, which is rare. It's a..." Cordelia squeezed her eyes shut in concentration for a moment. "Strike that, I don't recall the name, but I know what it's for. You use it to hold the yarn in place as you wind it into a ball." She gave a halfhearted shrug. "I'm the least knitterish of the group. I enjoy it, mostly, but I'm not passionate about it like most of the others. I use it more as a social activity, a break from everything else. I frequently knit on my own, but nothing more elaborate than a scarf or hat every now and then. But I've seen them use it, so I can attest it's not a murder weapon or anything."

Watson reared up, propping his forepaws on Leo's shoulder so he could sniff the purple contraption, his attention focused on the rubber handle.

"No, buddy, not for you." Leo held it out of reach.

"Oh, let him have it. Looks like a good chew toy, besides, Wanda was complaining about it anyway—it doesn't work as well as the metal kind. Plus, if Minnie sees him with it inside later, it'll give her something to gripe about." Cordelia smiled wickedly, her eyes twinkling. "Nothing makes her happier."

Lowering it once more, Leo offered it to Watson, who snapped it out of his hands, padded to the side of the van, and curled up and began to chew on the handle.

I wasn't finding anything of particular interest in the glove compartment, either. Mostly just forms from a rental company that showed that the group didn't own the vans themselves. "Speaking of Minnie, I couldn't help but notice that you're an interesting collection of women. Sounds like there are a lot of strong personalities, especially considering Alexandria."

"That's true. Part of what I enjoy." Cordelia pushed herself up from her kneeling place on the floorboards and plopped down on one of the seats, rubbing her knees. "Alexandria definitely had the most personality..." She shook her head, reconsidering. "No, she had the most *challenging* personality, that's a different thing. She didn't seem to like very many people, but she was talented, breathtakingly so."

That seemed to be the consensus about her and matched what I'd noticed. Even Angus, who'd had some sort of romantic relationship with her, considered her unlikable. "If Alexandria didn't care for people very much, why was she part of the knitting group?"

Cordelia cocked her head and narrowed her eyes. "In other words, is our knitting group a cover for this group? The... Irons family?"

Either she was very quick, or I hadn't been very covert. Or both.

She didn't give me a chance to answer. "If it is, I'd hardly tell you that, would I?" She chuckled again. Cordelia did that a lot—it was a soft, pleasing sound. Not at all fake or overdone. A sound that made me think she was content and at ease in her own skin.

My gut told me she was trustworthy, she wasn't a part of this. But she'd said herself that she was the least of the knitters, so maybe she wasn't aware of what the group truly was. Although... hadn't I noticed that the rest of them seemed to defer to her?

"I can't say Alexandria loved the group, but I think she was lonely, and she definitely enjoyed feeling superior with her skill. And while she was a frequent member, she missed a lot of our meetings and get-togethers. She was constantly going out of town at the drop of a hat, often without warning. You never knew if she was going to show up or not." Cordelia's tone was a little darker. "It was always easier, more relaxing at least, when she wasn't there."

I froze, staring at Cordelia.

She shifted uncomfortably. "What? Did I say something wrong?"

"No." I blinked, trying to shove the unease I felt away. "Just that she would come and go without warning. Without telling anyone." I felt Leo's gaze and looked past Cordelia to him. He offered an encouraging smile, one that said he was sorry, one that said he was there with me. With effort, I refocused on Cordelia. "The person I knew who was involved with the Irons family did the same thing. He was dependable and trustworthy to a fault, until he wasn't. He'd disappear instantly without warning and simply say it was personal business for a day or two and then show back up. It felt strange at the time, but..." I shrugged. "You know, you give excuses, decide things aren't your business or that you're being pushy or whatever. But now, looking back, it all seems so clear."

"I know what you mean." Cordelia sighed. "Wanda, Pamela, Betsy, and I were having the same conversation earlier, before Alexandria was killed. Even though none of it makes sense... it does. Things that we shrugged off as idiosyncrasies or just part of her abrasive personality suddenly are understandable, even if in an outlandish and unbelievable way. She wasn't pleasant, but I never would've thought she was a murderer."

"When did Alexandria move to...?" Suddenly I'd forgotten the name of the town.

"Willow Lane." Cordelia smiled encouragingly. "And she didn't. Alexandria was born there."

"Really?" That struck me as odd. "I guess my impression was that your town was small, a farming community."

"It is. At least partly. It's also got a decent influx of tourists during parts of the year. Nothing like here, I imagine, but we're located centrally enough between Kansas City, Branson, and Eureka Springs, which are all big destinations, that we catch some of the overflow. Especially during the spring and fall at the height of flowers and leaf changes."

I'd forgotten about the town Branson. We'd gone there once when I was a kid. It was like a different version of Nashville.

Leo spoke up from the back. "Do you know if Alexandria had any ties to Kansas City?"

She didn't hesitate. "Yes. Alexandria's parents divorced when she was young. I'm not sure how old, three or four maybe. Her dad moved to Kansas City. I wasn't close friends with her family, so I can't tell you the exact schedule or anything, but my impression was she would spend about a fourth of the time with him, during Christmas and summer breaks from school and such. That's not saying too much, though. A lot of us have connections to Kansas City. That's where we go when we have a large shopping trip to do or we want to see the lights. Branson and Eureka are bigger than Willow Lane, but they don't feel like going to a big city."

There it was again, that ribbon winding closer, pulling my father, Branson, and Estes closer together. Not to mention Alexandria, and maybe Angus and Darrell as well.

Cordelia leaned over, cracking open the side door of the van, letting in some fresh, cool air. "Did the person you knew have connections to Kansas City?" Her gaze was shrewd. "That seems to be important."

"He did. Yes. At least for a little while." My knees were starting to hurt as well, and I repositioned to the seat. For whatever reason, because some part of me already trusted the woman, or simply because I needed to release some of the tension and memories, I shared more than I normally would with Cordelia. "I grew up in Kansas City. My mother grew up in Estes, but I didn't move here until little over a year ago."

Cordelia hummed, as if in confirmation. "That explains it. I thought you felt like a Midwest girl."

"I am, at least in a lot of ways." I laughed. "But in nearly as many, I'm not. Even before I moved here, I think part of me had the Western sensibilities as well. Just a touch more liberal and... well, some of the expectations around women seem to be a little more... up to date here. But that could just be my relationship with my ex-husband talking." I forced a second laugh.

"You don't need to sugarcoat, honey." Cordelia cocked an eyebrow. "I'm a sixty-five-year-old woman who owns a farm. I've had more than my share of men telling me what I can or cannot do." She reached forward and smacked my arm. "And it gives me a lot of pleasure proving them wrong every time."

Leo's soft chuckle emanated from the back. When I looked at him, there was warmth and pride in his honey-brown eyes.

The sight made my breath catch. I'd seen that look before, but the eyes had been a different hue. Now that I'd seen it, I couldn't believe I hadn't caught on to the similarity before. Unlike my ex-husband, my father had instilled in me that there was nothing I couldn't do. That I was no weaker or less capable than any man in my life. And his eyes shone with pride and love every time they turned my way. Just like Leo. It was too much. Wonderful, but over-whelming and too much. I looked away, returning to Cordelia, but still needing to talk about my father. "My dad was a detective. He was killed several years ago, by the same group."

There was a gasp by the sliding door. "Page. You're Charles Page's girl?"

I looked over to see one of the other knitters, Betsy, standing there staring at me. Hearing his name took my breath away. "You knew my dad?"

She shook her head. "No. I didn't. But I had family there. I remember them talking about your father. It was a big deal. It even made the local news in Willow Lane. That bust in a warehouse gone wrong."

Cordelia gasped as well, looking from Betsy to me. "Oh. I do remember that." She reached forward to my arm once more, this time giving a soft squeeze. "I'm so, so sorry."

Betsy slid the door open farther and held a hand out toward Cordelia. "Help me up. I'm coming in." Once inside, she shut the door, shivering and rubbing her knee as well. "This cold is getting to me, and that officer woman has the whole van torn up over there and not letting anybody join her. I'd had enough."

"Have they found anything?"

"From the way that lady officer is reacting, you'd think so. Every little flick of lint is getting labeled and bagged." Betsy gave Leo a cursory glance. "But no, not a thing. I don't know what Alexandria hid in there, but..." Her eyes widened as she noticed

Watson chewing away, and then she looked toward Cordelia. "You're trying to give Wanda a heart attack, aren't you? Although, it's a small price to pay. Looks like you guys are being pretty neat. Having that officer in here messing up all the labels and categories might be more than Wanda can handle."

I couldn't care less at that point about categories, labels, or knitting tools. I lasered in on Betsy. "Do you know who Alexandria was visiting in Kansas City?"

"Not a clue." She shook her head definitively. "Alexandria was part of our knitting group, but never really a *part* of our knitting group, if you know what I mean. And she always had a hardness about her. I kept my distance." She shivered. "I'll never get that boy's image out of my head. Lying there with his throat slit. I knew Alexandria was cold, but I never would've guessed that." She lifted her brows toward Cordelia. "And poor Cassidy. I don't think she'll ever be the same. Such a nervous wreck. Poor thing. These are harder on the young ones. Not that it's easy on us, but we've seen enough hardships over the years that we can take it in stride."

I'd forgotten that Betsy and Cassidy had walked in when we'd discovered the body. Those details had all gotten carried away when Juliet came in and started screaming.

I'd also forgotten Cassidy for the moment. She hadn't seemed to be handling things very well. "Does…" I nearly stopped myself from asking, unsure if I should trust Betsy with what I was thinking, but then didn't see the harm. "Does Cassidy have a connection to Kansas City?"

"Oh, yes," Betsy answered instantly. Beside her I saw Cordelia's eyes widen, an expression that made me think some of her puzzle pieces were clicking together. "She dated a young man up there for a couple of years. Handsome thing, Tanner or Brody…" She wrinkled her nose. "Can't quite remember that either. One of those newfangled names. It ended badly. Cassidy was a mess for months."

That red ribbon just kept tying tighter and tighter.

SIXTEEN

"I really was starting to feel like a jailer down there." Katie plopped on the bed on her side of the room, then as if not quite relaxed enough, fell back so she was lying all the way down. "Between that Minnie woman and Anna, I've had my hands full."

"*Anna* is causing you problems?" I paused, sliding out of my clothes. As I'd shut the van's sliding door, an avalanche of snow fell off the roof, covering my hair, and somehow managing both to fall down the back of my sweater and snow pants. As soon as we walked in, I headed to the room to change, and Katie took advantage of Susan wanting to lecture the group—not having found any evidence in either one of the vehicles had put her in a foul mood.

Watson had stayed with Barry, as if he'd missed him desperately during our short time outside.

"Not problems per se, just..." Katie sighed,

"Well, you know Anna. She's got a million different theories about who killed Luca and Alexandria. She has no problem speculating aloud, even if the object of her current theory is sitting less than ten feet away. She's found some way to implicate every single staff member and each of the knitters. She even accused Gerald at one point."

I pulled a different sweater and a broomstick skirt out of my backpack, considering Anna's theories. She'd been right on other occasions—of course, given her high percentage of theories, she had to be correct sometimes. "Chances are she's on the right track with at least one of them. I can't see Gerald killing anyone, but he was up and about last night, and seemed a little jumpy when our paths crossed."

"Probably went out to his car to get more kombucha." Katie chuckled. "One of Anna's theories was that Gerald was having an affair with Alexandria. That was when you all were interviewing Angus, thankfully."

"Really? That's an interesting hypothesis. I suppose that could've happened. He might've been coming back from her cabin."

"You think?" Katie propped herself up on her elbows. "Alexandria didn't strike me as a very nice person, but did you see her? She was gorgeous. And Gerald is so much older."

"He's about the same age as Angus, and Alexandria and Angus had a..." I hesitated, trying to figure out a way to describe it, then gave up. "A thing."

"Yeah, but Angus is..." Katie hesitated that time, also seeming to search for words. "I don't know, intriguing a little bit, talented, kind of classy. Gerald..." She shuddered.

"That about sums it up." I agreed with her. I could see the allure of Angus, but Gerald was everything that drove me crazy about the good old boys club members all rolled into one. Yet... that ribbon seemed to be weaving around Angus, not Gerald. "Still, I'd say you were closer with the kombucha, especially since Carl was up and about last night as well. I don't suppose Anna threw his name out there?" As I looked in the mirror to fix my hair, I chuckled again. I couldn't imagine Anna tossing her husband's name in the ring as far as suspects, but I wouldn't entirely put it past her, either. "From the sounds of it, everybody and their dog were awake during the night last night. I saw several, and then according to Susan, Luca caught several more. She didn't mention Leo and me, so somehow we must've avoided Luca's spying camera, because I can't imagine Susan not rubbing it in our faces." Satisfied that my damp long hair wasn't going to turn into a frizzy mess, I turned to find Katie sitting straight up on the bed, gaping at me. I froze. "What?"

"You *and Leo* avoided Luca's camera?" Brown eyes narrowed suspiciously even as her lips began to curve into a smile. "You two were up in the middle of the night?"

"No. I..." *Crud!* I hadn't realized what I'd said. Somehow, I'd also managed to forget Katie didn't already know. "It wasn't the *middle* of the night."

Katie popped the rest of the way up, hurried across the room, grabbed my hands, and pulled me beside her as she plopped on my bed. "*Please* tell me you two have quit beating around the bush already. It's killing me."

I started to feign ignorance, or at least claim that we'd not been beating around the bush or anything else, but she wasn't wrong. Though it felt indulgent, considering there were two dead bodies within the past many hours, I allowed myself to have this moment with my best friend and angled toward her, feeling a touch like a giddy schoolgirl. "It's kind of unreal." Even as I spoke, my heart began to race pleasantly at the memory of us beside the fire.

"What is?" She smacked my arm impatiently.

"What's unreal? What happened? Tell me everything."

Telling everything, all the minute details, wasn't my style, Katie knew that, but... "We kissed. And..." My cheeks began to burn. "I just... *we* just know. You know?"

When Katie didn't respond immediately, I looked back up at her, finding her gaping once more.

"What?"

"What!" Katie practically screeched. "How can you even ask that? The two of you have been slower than frozen molasses since the day you met, and now you've suddenly gone from driving up here like the best of friends with me *yesterday* to being a thing within a couple of hours?"

"Well..." Her reaction threw me off, maybe seeing it from an outside perspective, as right as it felt, I had to admit it was rather a massive leap. "I suppose it was a bit fast."

Katie groaned and grabbed my arm. "Fast? Did you hear me? Glaciers move faster. But leave it to you to finally go for it, *really* go for it, when you decide to go for it."

"I *think* I understood that sentence." Some of my giddiness returned. "So you approve?" As soon as the question left my lips, I wished I could pull it back. I wasn't a giddy schoolgirl. I didn't require anyone's approval.

"Dear Lord, yes!" Katie was too quick to pull it back, and I was glad. She grew hesitant instantly, though. "So... you two are... together? Officially?"

I opened my mouth to speak but was lost for words. Were we official? What did that even mean? "All I know is while maybe it'll seem crazy to everyone, kind of does to me, it just feels right, like when the puzzle pieces finally click and my gut just knows something—*that's* how this is. It's kind of tilting my world out of whack, but at the same time... I just know. And when we kissed—" I chuckled again, self-consciously that time "—I'd have thought it would have been weird, that we were too good of friends, that it would've felt like relatives or something, but... it didn't. It felt right too, it felt... wonderful."

When Katie was silent again, I discovered her eyes brimming with unshed tears, her face shining, and then she launched across the space between us, wrapping her arms around my neck with such force that we fell over, causing the bed to squeak, and we got lost in happy laughter.

"Good grief! What took you so long?" Susan

growled as we entered the dining room. "Katie, take over again. And this time there's no talking at all. None." Susan looked back at three different groups of people spread throughout the dining room, pointing at each one individually. "I mean it! If no one's going to come clean, then we'll go one by one, and then repeat the process as many times as we have to." She sounded close to becoming unhinged. "No, no, Percival. I *don't* care if it's your anniversary. Dead bodies trump wedding vows or whatever." With a final shake of her finger, she whirled back around and stormed off toward the key room. She was nearly to the fireplace in the lobby before she looked back at me. "Are you coming or not, Fred? Leo's already got Darrell and your fleabag in the key room. But if you're done playing detective for once, take a seat."

Okay... it seemed she'd well and truly jumped over the line of becoming unhinged. I exchanged a quick glance with Katie, then hurried after Susan.

Thankfully, Leo was seated in the middle of the sofa, so Susan and I took our spots on either side. Watson licked my hand, then settled his rump on my boot and lay so that his forepaws were crossed on Leo's shoe, content to touch both of us.

Leo started to smile at me, but when his eyes met

mine, he paused as if seeing something in me. The corner of his lip turned up. "Everything good?"

I felt my own lip smile in return. "Very."

"Good grief, you two. Get a room." Susan scowled. "Actually, don't. That's a disgusting thought. But for crying out loud, tone it down. Today is horrible enough without having to deal with nausea issues." She whirled to Darrell, who was practically trembling in the hot seat. "Why were you sneaking around in the middle of the night last night?"

His eyes went wide, and he started to open his mouth.

"Nope!" Susan sliced her hand through the air. "Don't even try to deny it. I saw you on that weaselly Luca's phone. He caught you. Is that why you killed him? Tired of him snooping around, filming everyone behind their backs? Did he finally catch you in an incriminating situation? Were you the one with Alexandria at the van?"

Darrell flinched with every question Susan threw at him, and his fair complexion grew more flushed with each one as well. By the time she was done, his face was crimson. "I... no... I..." He shook his head violently. "No."

"No what?" Susan snarled, her top lip actually

pulling up over her teeth. "No, you didn't kill him because of the video, or you weren't by the van with Alexandria? Or no, there's a different reason you killed Luca?"

Leo spoke, his voice calm and soft, as if soothing a wild animal. "Why don't we try one question at a time? Like Officer Green said, Luca caught you moving around in the middle the night. What were you doing?"

Darrell seemed to relax somewhat, but his voice was barely more than a squeak. "Nothing. I just got up to... get water. And I... had a bad dream."

Susan groaned, loud and exaggerated. "You had a bad dream? How old are you? Five?"

Darrell glanced at the French doors, as if hoping someone would come to save him.

Susan clapped her hands, making him jump and look back at her. "Answer the question!"

"No! I'm not five!"

Susan flinched, thrown off, then groaned again and began to rub her temples. "I'm surrounded by idiots."

I laughed, I couldn't help it. It started as a soft chuckle and then something got a hold of me, and I started to laugh. Just the ridiculousness of the whole situation, all of it. It was all so preposterous, topped off with this handsome redheaded man—clearly terrified by Susan, not that I could blame him—proclaiming that he was not a five-year-old.

After a second, Leo joined in.

At our feet, Watson sat up, looking back and forth between us, tongue lolling as if he was in on the joke.

Susan simply glared, while Darrell looked as if we were crazy.

After a minute or so, I managed to get myself under control. And ridiculous or not, the laughter had helped. "Why don't we try this?" I leaned forward, looking intensely at Darrell and using a tone that fell somewhere between Susan's and Leo's. "I'm going to cut to the chase. There're too many coincidences to be believable in this situation. The Irons family is based in Kansas City. It shows up here, where there are also ties. There appears to be some sort of exchange or secret event happening in the middle of the night. And *you're* here, the only employee of Baldpate Inn who's not international. Not only that, but you're from the Ozarks, near the heart of this whole thing. Don't you think that's a little too much to be..." My words fell away as I studied the pure confusion and alarm over his face, which, in a way, truly transformed him into an overgrown child. Too much coincidence or not, I suddenly knew, without a doubt, we were wasting our time with Darrell. He had no clue what the Irons family was. "You don't know anything, do you?"

He shook his head, wide-eyed.

Leo and Susan both turned to look at me, their expressions as different from each other's as possible. Leo appearing somewhat surprised, but instantly believing me. Susan seemed as if she was about ready to rip my head off.

At that exact moment, the French doors burst open. "Me! He was with me."

Watson let out a yelp of surprise and jumped to attention at the outburst, and all of us turned to stare at the beautiful blonde rushing into the room.

Cassidy hurried to Darrell's side, and placed a hand on his shoulder, but didn't sit down, as if she was the protector he'd been waiting on. "Darrell was with me last night. I made him promise not to say. I didn't want people to think..." Her cheeks went scarlet as well, but she didn't look away. "Nothing happened between us. He was innocent. I'm not that kind of girl. But people would think..." She shook her head.

"She's *not* that kind of girl." Darrell found his

voice again. "We were just talking. Well... we might have kissed, but... that's all."

Though Cassidy seemed like even that much detail was humiliating, she nodded.

Beside me, Leo snickered, but then the sound cut off as if he'd bit his lip to stop it.

It took all I could do to not lose it.

"You mean..." Susan started, then let out a long angry breath before trying again. "You mean to tell me that Luca caught you heading to some midnight rendezvous with"—she fluttered her hand at Cassidy —"this Barbie doll knitter-wannabe?"

"Hey!" Darrell started to stand, apparently getting over his fear of Susan. "You can't—"

"That won't help." I stood, motioning for Darrell to sit, and focused on Cassidy. "You're dating Darrell?"

She hesitated. "Well... not exactly. We just met last night, but..."

I halted. "*Last* night?"

Darrel looked back up at her and took her hand. "But when you know, you know."

"Oh, good God." Susan truly did sound like she was battling nausea. "I don't know how much more of this I can take."

I ignored her, studying the two of them. "You

just met yesterday? From my understanding, don't you both live pretty close to each other?"

They nodded as one, both looking excited, and it was Darrell who spoke again. "That's part of it, like fate. So close to each other all this time and yet we meet here, of all places. When I get back home, I'm going to move to Willow Lane so I can be—"

"You're going to move?" Susan interrupted again, gesturing toward Cassidy. "You're going to *move*? For a woman you just met..." She checked her watch then seemed to give up. "Ten seconds ago?"

"Yeah." Darrell repeated his earlier sentiment. "When you know, you know."

Hadn't I just been saying the equivalent about Leo and myself? Although it'd taken us over a year to get to that point, not less than a day.

Cassidy beamed down at Darrell, her eyes filled with happy tears.

"But, Cassidy, what about—" I cut off my words when she looked at me. I'd been going to ask her about Kansas City. About the man she'd dated. Just like before, nothing clicked, my gut just knew. No matter the coincidence, no matter how the red ribbon seemed to be looping and tying, these two were the wrong pieces to the wrong puzzle. They weren't involved. They didn't know a thing.

SEVENTEEN

Carl scooted his chair nearer to the fire in the staff lounge and balanced his heavily laden plate on his legs. Reconsidering, he glanced around, discovered a decorative pillow on another chair, grabbed it, and plopped it on his lap to use as a table.

As the two of us had walked through the kitchen, he'd snagged a plate and piled it high. Though it was the exact same food as what everyone else was snacking on in the dining room, from the pleased expression on his face, he clearly felt as if he'd gotten something special.

When Carl judged himself appropriately situated, he peered over his glasses and smiled at me, once more reminding me of the perpetual Santa Claus with his bald head, white cottony beard, and cheerful girth. "I'm glad you're the one interrogating me, Fred. I was afraid it would be Susan. Sometimes

I get so flustered with her. I..." He shuddered, then propped his feet up on the hearth. "Well, who knows, I might just confess to a murder I didn't commit to get it over with."

I could almost see him doing that very thing. "I'm not interrogating you, Carl. There's no reason to be nervous."

Watson propped his forepaws up on the hearth as well, sniffing Carl's shoes, and whimpered.

"I don't think Watson knows that." Carl chuckled, started to lean forward to scratch Watson's head, but leaned back, as if it was too much effort. "Sorry, little man. I know Anna always has me get your favorite... food items..." He shot me a knowing wink, having successfully avoided Watson's favorite word. "But I'm all out at the moment."

Either understanding Carl's words, or not picking up any scent of the all-natural dog bone treat he so adored, Watson let out a huff, crashed back to the floor, and padded over to curl up under my chair.

After the rather disastrous interview with Darrell, Susan announced she'd had enough. She suggested the three of us split up to talk to the rest of the Estes Park crew. Susan had taken Gary into the key room, and Leo and Anna were on the far side of the kitchen.

As I watched Carl arranging chunks of cheese between two large slices of cornbread, crafting a makeshift sandwich, I couldn't help but feel like we were wasting our time. Carl wasn't entirely wrong. Interrogating was exactly what we were doing, but... it wasn't working, and I didn't think it was going to. The murders were connected to the Irons family. They had to be. Clearly, it wasn't like the three of us were going to be so intimidating to a member of the crime organization that they'd crack. Watson might be a little grumpy, but he was hardly threatening. I supposed there was a chance that someone outside of the Irons family might have incriminating information that they weren't aware of knowing, but I doubted it. From what I'd seen so far, they were too careful, and if someone had been privy to something so incriminating, they probably would've already been taken out of the picture.

Even so... I couldn't think of another approach.

"My goodness." Carl hummed happily, then spoke with his mouth full. "I've always loved Baldpate's cornbread. With all that I've eaten the past couple of days, you'd think I'd be sick of it, but I think I'm growing more obsessed by the moment." Still chewing, he lowered his partially eaten cornbread sandwich, opened it up and popped a few pepperoni slices from the salad bar on top of the cheese.

Might as well jump in. "Did Anna enjoy the cornbread for her midnight snack last night?"

"Anna?" He'd already had the sandwich raised partway to his lips, but jolted, looking at me wide-eyed. "Oh..." He looked away, toward Watson, then settled on the fire. "Right. Yes. The snack. Yes." He looked back to me. "Yes."

Carl was a world-class gossip, but not a good liar. I hadn't truly been attempting to catch him in a lie, I no more expected Carl being involved than I did Watson. But from the flush that crept over his already rosy cheeks, his nose might as well have grown a foot.

Obviously, Anna had *not* requested a midnight snack. Carl had seemed nervous and strange when he'd run across Watson and me reading in front of the fire—looked like Katie's theory was correct. "Were you sneaking out to get some of Gerald's kombucha? I know Anna doesn't approve."

"No! I have a bottle stashed in—" His eyes widened once more, and he snapped his mouth shut. The excuses flooding behind his eyes were so clear I nearly laughed. "I mean..."

"It's okay, Carl. I'm not going to tattle on you." I

did laugh, a little, at his relieved expression, but pushed forward anyway. "So what were you doing? After you went back upstairs, Gerald came in from outside. You really weren't meeting for kombucha?"

His relief faded, and he tried for offense, though he didn't quite succeed. "I thought you said this wasn't an interrogation."

I cocked my head at him, taken aback. Carl *did* have a secret. One that had nothing to do with kombucha, apparently. Maybe that shouldn't surprise me; everyone had secrets. It seemed Luca had a cell phone filled with other people's secrets. Suddenly, I wasn't sure I wanted to know what Carl's secret was. I liked him, considered him a friend. Considered Anna a friend. I didn't want there to be anything to jeopardize that. I knew that Carl hadn't killed anyone, but that didn't mean he was innocent.

"Don't look at me like that." Carl sounded hurt, guilty.

"Sorry." I could barely force myself to whisper. "I didn't mean to."

Though I hadn't even been trying, Carl cracked like an egg. "Fine. Fine. Just... don't tell Anna." He looked over my shoulder toward the closed door that was between the staff lounge and the kitchen as if she might be listening on the other side.

The sick knot in my stomach tightened. I didn't want to know this. Whatever it was, I didn't want to know this.

Even so, I nodded.

"I was meeting with Gerald. Or... was supposed to." Carl stopped again, peering over my shoulder once more, and then, for some odd reason, at the fire, before turning his earnest eyes back on me. "We were going to meet outside, under the deck, but when I found you and Watson, I... got the cornbread instead."

"You were meeting *Gerald*?" Relief flooded me. Though I hadn't even been aware of what I'd feared, I think some part of me expected him to say he was meeting up with Alexandria for some sort of tryst.

He nodded guiltily. "You can't tell Anna." I started to cut him off, to keep him from sharing whatever it was. There was no way he'd been meeting with Gerald to plan murder, so it was better for me not to know, I didn't want to keep things from Anna. Before I could, Carl got going, as if relieving a weight on his soul to a priest. "I'm relocating some money, quite a bit of money, in an investment opportunity that Gerald presented me.

He thinks it can quadruple its profits within a year."

"Investments?" Again a wave of relief. Not an affair, nothing I'd feel I'd have to tell Anna. The relief was short-lived. I'd heard more than one story of a spouse making financial decisions without the other's input only to ruin both of their futures. "Wait a minute, Carl, what kind of investment? How much are you talking about?"

He shrugged, again not meeting my gaze. "A good chunk of change. I'm only taking money out of my retirement, not accounts that Anna and I have together."

That was something, I supposed. Still... "This is an investment idea of Gerald's?"

Carl nodded, looking hopeful suddenly, misinterpreting the disbelief he'd heard in my tone. "Yeah. If you want to join in, you can."

Not in a million years would I throw a penny at any idea Gerald Jackson had. That was beside the point. Something didn't add up. There were a million ways he could speak to Gerald without Anna's knowledge. "Why were you two meeting outside in the middle of a blizzard? Doesn't Gerald have his own room?"

Again his cheeks pinked in embarrassment.

"Yeah, but it's next to Angus's, and there's a door connecting the two. Gerald was afraid Angus would overhear."

It still didn't add up. "Why wouldn't Gerald want Angus to know?"

"Angus helps Gerald with everything." Relief flooded Carl's voice at finally being asked an easy question. "Angus... well, you know... he's smart, talented, handsome." The pink deepened yet again. "Has a gorgeous girlfriend, or... did." Carl offered an obligatory grimace.

I nodded for him to continue.

"Angus is Angus." He shrugged self-consciously. "We wanted to prove that we could do this on our own. Impress him, you know? It's not like he'd be missing out when it goes well. He already has a fortune."

"He does?" That was news to me, not that I was privy to people's financials.

Carl simply nodded as if that should've been common knowledge.

Maybe it was, perhaps I was just looking into things. Angus always appeared well dressed and cultured. Though I wouldn't have thought of it unprompted, I could see why his friends would feel a little intimidated about him. Still... a fortune? From a yarn store in Estes Park? However... Angus had mentioned in the past that some of his knitted artwork was in galleries, and the price tags of the ones he had for sale at his shop were staggering. Even so, that ribbon continued to wind a little tighter.

I leaned forward, the chair squeaking. "Did you run into Angus last night?"

"Uhm... no?" Carl flinched, looking puzzled. "That was the whole point. Gerald and I were meeting outside because Anna was in my room, of course, and Angus was too close to Gerald's."

Right... Angus had been asleep in his room. Or had he waited until Gerald fell asleep and met Alexandria by the vans? "I'm a little surprised you guys had to worry about him. You said yourself Angus had a beautiful girlfriend. Why wouldn't he be with Alexandria in her cabin?"

"You know, I wondered that too." All worry was forgotten in Carl's tone. "If *I* had a girl who looked like..." The worry-free Carl was short-lived. He balked at his own words, pulling his feet off the hearth and leaning toward me with panicked sincerity. "I am not jealous of Angus and Alexandria. I love Anna. I don't need a pretty girlfriend. Nor do I want one."

"Carl, I didn't—"

"I'm serious." Carl leaned closer, the decorative pillow falling to the floor as he discarded the plate of food on the hearth before grabbing my hands and locking his gaze on mine. "I *love* Anna. I've never betrayed her, and never will."

I tried again. "Carl, I really wasn't—"

"Sure, she's a little sharp at times, a little mean, but that's just her way." Carl squeezed my hands. "She's not as thin as when we got married, neither am I! She's the mother of my children. We spent decades building our business together. And when things happened with Billy at Christmas..." Emotion thickened his voice. "When we found out our son hurt..." He squeezed his eyes shut for a second, but then his hard gaze was back. "I wouldn't trade Anna for a billion Alexandrias. Not even for a second."

Carl's words were so heartfelt, so sincere, that it made my eyes sting. I squeezed his hands back. "I know." Even though I'd worried what I was about to hear around that very area only a few moments before. In a lot of ways they were a ridiculous mess, the two of them. But they couldn't be better matched. "I know you love Anna. And I know she loves you."

He studied me for a second, more intensely than Carl had looked at me before. Finally he relaxed, released me, and after getting his plate once more, sat back, satisfied. "Good. Because I do."

At the movement, Watson poked his head out from under my chair and peered up at us. Convinced nothing was amiss, Watson returned to his nap, letting out a contented snort.

When Carl had taken a couple more bites of the cornbread, cheese, and pepperoni sandwich, I tried again. "Do you have a theory on why Angus wasn't with Alexandria last night?"

"Yeah. Well, not a theory. I *know*." Carl finished swallowing. "They had a disagreement. Angus was irritated that she'd shown up with her knitting group and ruined our friends' anniversary party. He really cares about your uncles. We all do. It was supposed to be their special night, and then Alexandria and her knitting friends, half of which see Angus as a rock star, come blundering in and—" He sucked in a breath. "Fred! You cannot think that Angus would hurt her. Or that boy. He is *not* a murderer."

I didn't respond, trying to piece through things.

"I'm serious," Carl continued, filled with as much sincerity as when he'd spoken about Anna. "Why, Angus is one of the best people I've ever met. Anna and I were struggling with Cabin and Hearth after a really horrible tourist season a few years ago.

He gave us a loan, interest-free. Told us we didn't even need to worry about paying him back if we couldn't. He's done similar for many people. He's a good man, a great friend, and a... better man than me." The hero worship was so evident, Carl might as well have been talking about Superman.

"I'm not saying he isn't, Carl." Angus never struck me as Superman, but the few interactions we'd had made me feel like he was a genuinely good guy. "But it's hard to ignore that a lot of these details are swirling around him. He—" When a look mixed with horror and denial crossed Carl's face, I changed tactics. "I'm sure you're right. I'm probably... just desperate to solve this case."

Carl's eyes narrowed, and then he seemed satisfied. "Can't blame you for that, but you're wasting your time looking at Angus. He's a good man, Fred. Ask anybody. A good, good man."

"I know." That time, I leaned toward Carl. "It's my turn to ask for a favor. Don't mention my suspicions to Angus, okay?" Even as the words left my lips, I knew they were pointless. Carl could swear up to high heaven, but it was a promise I knew he couldn't keep. The juicy tidbit, to him and his wife, was a morsel so delectable, that the only way to enjoy it was to share it. Even if he promised, my suspicions would get back to Angus, maybe today, maybe in a week, maybe in a month. I'd just have to hope whenever it was, I'd figure out if Angus was connected to the Irons family *before* that occurred.

Seemingly unaware of his own limitations, Carl barely had to consider. "Of course. I care about you, Fred. You know that. I'm not going to spread gossip and rumors about you. And I also know it's only part of why you're so good at all of this. You have to ask the hard questions."

"Thank you, Carl." Even though I knew he wouldn't be able to help himself, I appreciated it.

"Can I ask the same of you?" He didn't sit back. "Will you keep my secret from Anna? When the investment pays off, she'll be so happy."

I almost said yes instantly, both because it wasn't my business and in hopes that it would help him stay silent a bit longer. But my gut clenched at the thought. Maybe he was right, maybe the investment was sound, even with Gerald's involvement, and I didn't know his and Anna's financial situation, either. But... he'd just stated they'd needed help not too long before. I settled on a compromise. "How about this, Carl? If for some reason I feel inclined that I should let Anna know about Gerald's"—I nearly said scheme—"plan, I'll let you know first.

Give you a chance to tell her yourself. Will that work?"

He seemed like he was about to argue, then nodded reluctantly. "I suppose. Thank you."

As Carl finished his strange sandwich, I tried to come up with some sort of scheme of my own that would help me reveal Angus's involvement one way or another.

EIGHTEEN

The sunset glowed pale purple over the landscape of rugged mountains and forests of trees blanketed in snow. The shadows extended over the valley, the darkness of where I knew Estes Park to be only confirming that no one had regained power yet.

Susan's loud, yet muffled, curse drifted from the dining room. Watson lifted his head from where he was curled up beside me, glaring in the noise's direction and then glowering up at me as if irritated that I had yet to fix the situation.

"I think she's starting to crack." I rubbed the pale pink spot on his nose earning a deeper scowl. "Not that I can blame her." I truly had been impressed with Susan for much of the day, but after hours of interviews with not a single insight or lead, we were all frazzled. When Susan suggested doing a second round with everyone, I told her I was finished, that I couldn't help but feel we were wasting our time.

The fireplace called to me from the lobby, but it was too close to Susan's group interrogation, so I'd taken refuge on the love seat by a window in the key room. I wasn't surprised that the interviews led nowhere. We were dealing with the Irons family, after all—why would they crack under a lowly small-town police officer, a park ranger, and a bookshop owner?

I looked out at the beautiful sunset once more, then scanned the thousands of keys hanging from the ceiling. They were a marvel. Keys from all over the world, from all sorts of people, from foreign royalty to a small child in Wisconsin. Thousands of strangers connected by this one room, this century-old log cabin resort. That had to be the answer—connection. There was some connection we were missing, one that wouldn't come out simply because the three of us lined up on a sofa with a corgi at our feet while we drilled question after question after question. The answer was here somewhere. It had to be.

Unless... like Leo's current theory... the murderer wasn't among us anymore. The other figure beside Alexandria at the van had come and gone. The notion still didn't sit right with me. If there was some outside person involved with Alexandria, they were probably part of the Irons family as well, so why kill her?

Watson stretched, pressing his back against my thigh as he groaned contentedly, already dreaming.

I'd brought Alexandria's sketchbook with me. After adjusting the lantern on the side table, I opened the pages. I'd already looked through it once, but decided to go through one more time. Inside the front cover was a list of twenty-three dates. No description, no explanation, just dates. Then a blank page, like in a published book, then the drawings.

Angus was right, Alexandria's skill was remarkable. Every single sketch was beautiful. Each had depth and texture. It didn't matter if the subject was animal, flora, or people—they were lifelike. It seemed offensive somehow, that someone with so much talent, who could create things of such beauty, would waste their life with crime. Would kill a young man who was barely more than a child.

The sketch of Alexandria and Branson was near the front of the book, so I came to it quickly, and I paused, studying him. Though the drawings were charcoal, or lead, I couldn't tell, even in absence of color, the details were so fine I could practically see the green of his eyes looking at me from the page. His lips so lifelike that I could hear his whisper to Watson that'd he'd always keep his mama safe. And he had. Though nearly everything said or done had been a lie, that was a promise he'd kept. He'd turned my world upside down, but he'd also saved my life.

Studying the younger version of his face, I realized I didn't hate him, that I was barely even angry at him. More than anything, I wished I could close the book and have him disappear. Have the whole Irons family and their effect on my life vanish.

I started to turn the page, but then noticed something at the end of Alexandria's swirling signature. A date. The third of June, fourteen years earlier. I flipped back to the inside cover. Sure enough, it matched the very first date on the top of the list. All thoughts and ponderings of Branson vanished as a shot of excitement coursed through me.

I began to flip the pages, discovering dates on every single drawing and matching some of them with the list.

"You doing okay in here?"

I looked up, startled. I hadn't heard the squeak of the French doors.

At the sound of Leo's voice, Watson sprang from

sleep, leaped off the love seat, and bounded toward Leo.

He stepped in, closed the door behind him, and knelt to greet Watson, but kept his concerned gaze on me.

"Yeah, I'm..." I glanced around, realizing I'd lost track of time. The sunset was long gone, the dark sky filled with stars over the snow outside the window. The corners of the key room were pitch-black, and strange key-shaped shadows flickered over the ceiling and the walls. "I guess I was gone awhile."

With a final pat on Watson's head, Leo stood across the room. "Don't worry, you didn't miss much. Although I think we're about to have a rebellion if Susan makes everyone continue to stay in the dining room. It's a long time in one place." He started to sit beside me and paused halfway, noticing the sketchbook in my lap, then finished, looking at me with concern. "Are you okay?"

Before I could answer, Watson jumped up, filling the small space between us.

As one, we both lowered our hands to stroke him, and our fingers touched.

There was a jolt, a little shot of electricity that was both unnerving and pleasant. I remembered feeling it when Leo and I had touched months and months ago. I wondered at that... how had we not felt that every time? Before the question even finished forming I knew the answer. I'd avoided touching Leo as much as possible. Whether that choice had been intentional or unconscious, I wasn't entirely sure. I pulled my hand back at the contact, out of reflex, then lowered it again, covering his hand where it lay on top of Watson's side. The jolt happened again, though it was sharp and quick, giving way to a pleasant buzz. I lifted my gaze to Leo's, which glowed nearly yellow in the candlelight.

"Yes. I'm okay." I stroked my thumb over the back of his hand. "Very."

A relieved smile crossed his handsome face, and he kept his voice low. "Several times today I wondered if I'd imagined things last night. I know I didn't, but it's just hard to believe that we're finally..." He ended with a small shrug.

Finally. Like I'd kept him waiting. Which... I supposed, I had. "Did you know this would happen? It was just a matter of time?"

"No." He chuckled self-consciously. "I'm sure I'm supposed to say yes, that I did. It would be more romantic that way. If I could claim I knew we were fated to be together, that it was destiny, or written in the stars or something. But I didn't. In fact—" His gaze darted to the sketchbook, as if expecting to see Branson's face there. He didn't. It was opened to a drawing of a tractor in a field of sunflowers, framed on one side with a large tree, its branches stretching over the top. He looked back up. "I gave up for a while. When it looked like you'd made your choice, you *had* made your choice. I decided I'd have to be content with being your friend. Even so, it wasn't like I could move on." Another chuckle, followed by a grimace. "As I said, not the most romantic of answers."

"Actually, it is." The warmth inside burned brighter than any lantern ever could. "I don't know if I believe in destiny or fate anyway. But I..." My words caught, the weight of the sketchbook on my lap suddenly heavier, causing me to reevaluate what I was about to say, and in that moment, I realized just how true it actually was. "I trust this. Maybe because of the wait, because of our friendship. I trust... *us*."

Smiling, he leaned closer and kissed me softly, tenderly.

Disrupted, Watson grunted, and hopped off the love seat, casting an irritated glare at Leo.

I laughed. "I didn't even know he could look at you that way."

Leo barely spared Watson a glance. "I'll survive." And then he kissed me again.

"See here..." I flipped back and forth from the inside cover of the sketchbook to various pages. "These dates correspond. Every single date goes with the drawing."

Leo had scooted closer, one of his arms over my shoulders. Watson had joined us and snored from his curled-up spot on the other side. Leo used his free hand to turn a few pages. "But not all the drawings have dates on the list."

"Right." I'd noticed that as well but hadn't been able to figure out the reasoning of it, but it was important. I could feel an answer there. Though if it had to do with the current murderers, the Irons family, or something else, I had no idea. "There has to be something significant about the pictures on that list. But I don't see any common theme through them. There's a few that are people's faces, but most are landscapes or still-life studies. Even those don't have a unifying theme either. Some are rural, others are cities or large buildings, there's even a couple that are landmarks from other countries."

"But the first one on the list is the drawing of

Alexandria and Branson." Even though the way Leo said it wasn't a question, I nodded. He continued. "The most recent on the list was two weeks ago."

I flipped to it. "Yeah. This drawing of Niagara Falls. I don't want to start the interrogations again, but I'm going to see if any of the knitters know if Alexandria was there two weeks ago, or sometime recently. It wouldn't be definitive, but it would indicate that this was like a diary of some sort, places she's been, people she's with."

"Seems reasonable." Leo reached over once more, flipping through the pages, not stopping on any one in particular. "It's strange that this goes back fourteen years. It's not *that* big of a book. For an artist, why would she make this last so long?"

I hadn't thought of that, but an answer came quickly, right or wrong. "From what Angus says, it sounds like knitting was her first love, her medium of choice. Even though these are exceptional, maybe she didn't draw all that frequently."

The French doors burst open again, and Watson, as before, lunged off the chair, this time giving a growl and bark.

"Oh, calm down, drama queen." Percival entered with a flourish and halted a few steps into the room, gaping at Leo and me.

Leo scooted over and took his arm from my shoulders.

Cocking his head, his eyes shrewd, Percival perched a hand on his hip as a huge smile lit his face. "Well... it's *about* time. You two were so slow that Gary and I were considering having an intervention."

Embarrassment flooded me for a moment as I felt like a teenager being caught by their parent bursting into the room. Shoving it aside, I reached over, took Leo's hand, and looked at him for confirmation.

He merely smiled, gave a squeeze, and turned to Percival. "I think you and Gary should still do it. I've never had an intervention. Could be fun. And knowing you two, there'd be glitter."

Percival sucked in an exaggerated gasp. "Stereotype much?" He shook his head in mock disgust at Leo and looked at me, shaking his finger. "You better hold on to this one, my lovely niece. A handsome man with a smart mouth is a catch." He glared down at Watson. "Not to mention he's good with your furball of attitude."

Leo chuckled, and though it was quiet, at the end, I caught a sigh of contentment. Happily, I realized that underneath the buzz of nerves and excitement around it all, that was how I felt as well—

content, at peace. I most definitely had never felt that with Branson, and… looking back, I didn't think I'd ever experienced it with my ex-husband, either.

Fate, destiny, or whatever, that was a good sign.

"Hurry up!" Percival pulled my attention back, as he waved us onward. "Murders or not, it's still Gary's and my anniversary, and it's time to party." He grimaced. "Maybe not party, since there's no electricity, no music, and we'll be eating the same food we've had for two days, delicious though it is, but it's a party nonetheless."

"Really?" Leo stared, disbelieving. "Susan gave her permission?"

"Permission?" Percival practically shrieked. "Honey, I don't need her permission. I've had enough. I stood up and said as much. Of course, she sputtered and threatened and whatnot…" He rolled his eyes exaggeratedly. "I told her that if she wanted to stop it, she'd have to shoot me."

"I'm kind of surprised she didn't."

Percival nodded at me sagely. "Honestly, I am too." He motioned for us to follow again. "So hurry up. Enough of this. If there really is a murderer in our midst, it's all the more reason we should grasp at living in the moment. And now, I have this wonderful juicy gossip of you two to share with the entire group. Talk about an anniversary present!" With a whirl, he headed back the way he came.

"Oh Lord. I'm so sorry." I started to rush after him, but Leo caught my hand. I turned to look at him.

He was hesitant, but the look in his eyes was sincere. "I don't care if everyone knows, if you don't."

Though it wasn't my style, I discovered I rather liked the idea of sharing my excitement.

NINETEEN

"Announcing... Mr. and Mrs. Winifred Page!" Percival had barely stepped one foot into the lantern-lit dining room before trilling out his announcement, then swept aside and gestured toward Leo and me with the twirling gesture. "That's right, Leo, you're taking *her* name. It's time to turn the patriarchy on its head."

Both of us halted, as did the rest of the room, at least the Estes Park side. Watson trotted forward a few feet and looked back quizzically.

After a second, Anna screamed, stood, and clapped her hands. "You're married?"

"Oh, for crying out loud," Susan muttered, and leaned against the curling iron lip of the bathtub salad bar as she rubbed one of her temples.

"No..." Leo came to his senses before me and laughed nervously. "Not married. We're just..." At a loss for words, it seemed, he looked at me, then simply held out his hand. We'd only dropped our grip moments before as we passed the lobby fireplace.

I took it again.

Another wave of silence, and then the Estes Park crew began to cheer and clap and holler. After a few seconds, the knitters and the staff joined in, though they seemed more confused than anything.

Though it felt like my cheeks were about to burst into flames, I couldn't help but giggle at their response and feel completely wrapped in their love. I found Mom's gaze from where she'd been talking with Zelda. Tears were already streaming down her cheeks as she made her way across the dining room and wrapped me in a hug. Typically I would've found it a little overdramatic, but... I was happy, and so was she.

Before I knew it, Leo and I were swept up in a tidal wave of congratulations.

From just outside the group, Susan threw up her hands in exasperation. "Good grief! It's not like you two announced your engagement or that you're having a baby, or did something important like solving cancer... or a murder."

Barry had just finished kissing me on the cheek,

and he dashed toward her, arms wide. "Come on now, we needed some good news, celebrate with us!"

One of her hands instantly went to the holster of her gun and the other shot out in front of her. "If you even *think* of hugging me, you crazy old man, there'll be another murder."

Nonplussed, Barry crashed into her, wrapping her sturdy frame in his long, lanky arms. At their feet, Watson pranced around, ready and willing to play any game Barry found entertaining.

Though Susan glowered at me over Barry's shoulder, I thought I caught a hint of a grin.

Within half an hour, Lisa and the staff had brought out more food. For the first time, maybe because of the celebratory spirit Percival had prompted, all three groups mingled together around the dining room. After the food was delivered, even some of the members of the staff dispersed among the rest of us.

Susan shared a table with Angus, Gerald, Barry, and my uncles. Probably sensing that Mom wanted some time with me, Leo joined them after a bit. From the intensity of their expressions, I assumed they were debating either the murders, or how we were going to get through the night safely when there might be a killer among us.

Not concerned about such issues, Watson lay on the floor between Barry's and Leo's chairs, looking back and forth at them in adoration, his little knob of a tail wagging happily.

Cordelia and Wanda had joined Katie, Mom, and me at our table. They'd seen us looking through Alexandria's sketchbook and were curious. Cordelia angled the drawing of Alexandria and Branson toward Wanda. "I'm certain I've never seen him. I think I'd remember. He'd stick out in Willow Lane."

Wanda cocked an eyebrow and tapped the page. "*He'd* stick out anywhere. He looks more like a movie star than a policeman."

It was an apt description. Leo and Branson were both handsome. But where Branson was more Hollywood perfection, almost uncomfortably so, Leo's beauty was more approachable, and maybe more alluring because of it.

"Well, we know for certain he was in Kansas City. He said as much to Fred." Mom glared at Branson's image, nowhere near being ready to forgive him for his deception. "I don't know if it matters if he was ever in Willow Lane or not. He was close, and knew Alexandria, clearly."

"What a waste." Katie sighed in disgust beside me.

"I agree." Mom nodded fervently. "That man is nothing but a waste."

"No, not Branson." Katie faltered. "I mean... I'm not defending him, but I meant Alexandria." She gestured toward the sketchbook. "She was a remarkable artist. I know it's different from baking, but it kills me seeing an artist so talented waste it all."

"You should see what that girl could knit." Cordelia shook her head in disbelief. "It was almost aggravating. I'd be struggling to knit so that it resembled anything recognizable, and she'd come along and craft something in a matter of hours that would take your breath away. Unfortunately, she knew it. She was always superior to everyone."

"In addition to skill, she was structured." Wanda nodded sagely. "She was organized, scheduled, and disciplined." She flipped to the inside cover. "Just look at these dates. Handwritten, but they're perfectly neat and straight, as if formatted on a computer."

Cordelia shot a knowing look at her friend. "It was always your favorite aspect of her."

"It was *my only* favorite aspect of hers." Wanda tapped the list. "It was her only soothing quality."

I'd forgotten that Wanda was the one who'd labeled all the yarn supplies. It made sense she'd connect to that characteristic of Alexandria.

"And you think the pictures that correspond with the dates are the important ones?" Katie angled the sketchbook her way. "Like a diary or something?"

"Exactly. They must..." Katie's words replayed through my mind. *A diary*. I'd thought the same thing when I'd perused it earlier, but as I pulled the book back and began flipping through the pages, checking the drawings with a date list again, it clicked. "I think it's a kill list."

The entire table turned toward me.

I flinched at the attention but reiterated the sentiment. "The dates. I bet they correspond with the times she murdered someone."

"Why?" Katie looked from me to the sketchbook and back to me again.

"Mostly a feeling." I shrugged. "But, it would be a sort of diary. Like you said."

Katie's eyes widened, looking excited, then almost sounded apologetic when she spoke again. "That makes sense as the first date matches the drawing of her and Branson."

The thought made my blood run cold. "Why do you think that?"

"I kind of wonder if he trained her. Maybe that was the day of her first kill." Her eyes met mine. "It might've been part of their relationship."

I refocused on the picture and considered Katie's words, combining her theory with mine. Part of me wanted to dismiss it, knowing about some of the crimes Katie's parents had committed, slough it off as nothing more than her projecting. But... as I studied the drawing, I felt the truth of it. I couldn't say what, but as Katie said, some instinct suggested it was the right track. I began flicking through the sketchbook again, finding the drawings that corresponded with the dates. "So maybe the ones of places are where she killed. A farm with the tractor, a little cottage, Niagara Falls. And the still lifes..." I flipped through the pages again. "A stack of books, a sleeping dog, an antique lamp... They're what? Things that she observed during the murder? I don't know. That seems a little far-fetched."

Mom pulled the book toward her, studying it as she addressed me. "Your father always said most of the killers he went after, at least the ones who'd killed a few times, ones that required planning, always kept some sort of record or souvenir. This could have been Alexandria's." As she spoke, Mom's finger trailed down the list, stopping about three-fourths of the way down. "Goodness, if we're right, that means she killed someone on Valentine's Day. That seems especially cold."

It was such a comment my mother would make. Valentine's Day was nothing more than just another commercialized day to me. To her, it signified romance and gentility. "Mom, I doubt—"

"Valentine's Day?" Cordelia stiffened, and her voice dipped to a whisper. She leaned closer to my mother. "Does it have the year?"

Mom angled the sketchbook toward Cordelia. "Yes. Right here. It was—"

"Oh." Cordelia gasped and looked over at her friend. "Wanda. 2012."

Confusion flared in Wanda's expression, and then her face went slack with understanding. "No. She couldn't have."

Mom, Katie, and I exchanged glances, but before any of us could ask, Cordelia had pulled the sketchbook toward her and was flipping through the pages. "You said there was a drawing of a tractor?"

"Yes. It's in the middle of this big sunflower field." I leaned across the table, getting ready to help her get to it, but Cordelia found it and gaped.

Beside her, Wanda's eyes widened, and two of them exchanged a look. As one, they both twisted in their chairs toward a table with a couple of the other knitters.

Overhead, the lights flickered, went out, flickered again.

The room went still.

Then the lights came on again, and this time stayed. The hum of electrical items began to purr in the distance.

"Oh, look!" Anna cried out from across the room and pointed through the French doors toward the glassed-in porch. Everyone followed her gesture, and there, glistening far away in the night, sheltered by the mountains, was the toy-sized Estes Park glittering and sparkling in the snow.

The entire room began to cheer. Everyone, except for our little table.

TWENTY

"The light is wonderful. Even so, I'm going to have to increase my prescription when we get home." Betsy adjusted her glasses and held up the blanket she was knitting. "Counting stitches by lantern light did irreparable damage. I don't know how they did it back in the days before electricity."

"We got up when the sun did and went to bed the same way. We had a natural rhythm to things." Minnie scowled across the small group. "It's you young ones who try to change the world to fit your whims, instead of going with the way the good Lord intended."

Betsy laughed. "I don't think anyone has called me young in thirty years." That time, she looked over the brim of her glasses. "And you're hardly older than electricity, Minnie."

Minnie grunted some comeback, but I didn't

catch it. I was too captivated staring at Betsy from where Susan, Watson, and I sat across the lobby.

"Quit staring. It's like you're trying to give it away." Susan nudged me hard with her elbow and hissed. "I barely agreed to this harebrained scheme of yours. Don't make me regret it."

A warning growl rumbled in Watson's chest.

Susan leaned forward and hissed to him as well. "Hush up, fleabag. Your momma is safe with me."

I flinched at her words and stared at her. There'd been many hard exchanges between the two of us in the past, but that comment seemed low, even for her. Especially when our relationship had been improving.

At my expression, Susan flinched right back. "What?"

I studied her for half a second, then relaxed. She hadn't meant anything. It had just been a coincidence. There was no way she'd known Branson used to say those exact words to Watson. "Nothing."

She narrowed her eyes at me, but didn't say anything, and we returned to looking through the sketchbook while eavesdropping on the knitters.

"Now, Katie." Angus spoke up from his spot of honor in the group. "Try not to hold your knitting needles so tightly. It's like kneading. The more relaxed you are with it, the better the bread will turn out."

"This is *nothing* like baking bread." Though Katie was only taking part in Angus's impromptu knitting lesson in pretense, the frustration was clear in her voice. At any other time, I probably would've laughed at my best friend. She hated not being top of the class in anything, and it seemed knitting wasn't coming naturally.

"Try this, dear." Mom reached over and adjusted the knitting needles in Katie's fingers.

"You're a natural, Phyllis." Angus peered over at what Mom had been working on. "We might have a new master knitter in the making."

"No, I don't think so." Mom waved him off, though she flushed happily at the praise. She'd insisted on being part of the ruse, saying that Katie and I always had all the fun. "Knitting is pretty and all, but I miss my crystals. I think I'll stick with jewelry making."

"Oh, Phyllis." Angus clucked affectionately. "There's many ways to incorporate crystals into knitting. We'll do a few private lessons when we get back. I'll open a whole new world to you."

Susan huffed out an impatient breath. "This is taking forever. Why did I listen to you again?"

Instead of answering, I nudged her with my elbow as she had me moments before.

In truth, the plan had only been partly mine. After Cordelia and Wanda had explained what the tractor drawing had revealed to them, my first inclination had been to have a confrontation then and there. Both of the women had negated that impulse, saying that if they were right, a direct accusation would be the last thing to prompt a confession.

Pamela issued a long, contented sigh. "I must say, there's nothing more soothing than knitting." She smiled graciously at Katie. "At least when you get the hang of it. Until then it's extremely frustrating. It took me a while. But once your brain can let go and allow your fingers to take over, it helps all the cares of the world fade away." She sighed again, dramatically. Too much so, she was too obvious. Beside me, I felt Susan stiffen, clearly having the same thought. Pamela shifted her focus from Katie to Betsy. "Not to mention that it helps get through the hard times in life, doesn't it, dear?"

Betsy looked to Pamela as she responded, her knitting needles not missing a beat. "It's true. It's a little like prayer. During the rough moments, or the rough years, you get lost in the stitches, each one healing your heart a little more than the last."

"I found the same thing to be true," Angus chimed in, his easy tone more natural than Pamela's. "Even now, I'm finding my heart a little more at ease, having the chance to return to this familiar comfort. It doesn't take away the loss, but it helps."

"She was important to you, wasn't she?" Cordelia delivered her prompt as naturally as Angus had set her up.

"She was." He hesitated for just the right amount of time, and when Angus spoke, he infused the perfect amount of anger into his sorrowful tone. "Alexandria wasn't who I thought she was, and I've not begun to grasp that fully, but her loss cuts me deeply. She was a—"

"I'm sorry." Minnie cut in, her tone harsh. "Are you actually lamenting that woman?"

Beside me, Susan started to stand. I gripped her knee, urging her to stay in place.

Angus didn't even flinch. "I am. Like I said, she might not have been who I thought she was, but the persona she presented to me was real. To me."

Minnie sniffed, unimpressed. "Seems to me you should be counting your lucky stars, not mourning someone like that." Her words were slightly slurred, bringing to mind whatever Susan had seen on the recordings that made her think Minnie might be hiding a drinking problem. "You could've ended up with your neck slit like that nosey young whipper-snapper."

"That only increases my ache. To know that a woman I cared about so deeply not only had a double life but was so cold, so cruel. That she could so easily take a life." Though I'd been hesitant to include Angus, given my suspicions, he proved it had been the right call, not only hitting the exact right note in the emotion to his voice, but seamlessly leaping to the heart of our setup. "I can't help but think back on our time together. All the long evenings we spent knitting together. Talking about our lives, comparing stories and experiences."

Betsy leaned across Wanda to pat Angus's arm sympathetically.

For once, it looked like Angus was thrown off, but only for a moment. Holding the knitting needles and the piece he was working on with one hand, he patted Betsy's hand. "I shared my favorite spot in the world with her. This beautiful pool way back in the mountains that, during the spring snowmelt, has three different waterfalls flowing into it." He smiled at Betsy as she pulled her hand away. "I shared that with someone I thought was a kindred spirit, a trusted friend and... companion."

Betsy offered a tight smile in return.

"I'm sure some of the moments you two shared were real." Unlike her sister, Cordelia delivered her prompt flawlessly. "Even in the darkest of hearts, I'm sure there are some light areas. Some semblances of the innocent child they were. Maybe you were a symbol of goodness to Alexandria. Perhaps she let you see the light she tried to bury in her own heart."

"Good grief, Cordelia." Minnie sounded thoroughly disgusted. "When did you get to be such a sap? Carrying on about a murderess? For crying out loud, Alexandria was barely likable to begin with. Now that we know the truth, there's no need to sugarcoat what she really was."

"I hate to say it, but I rather agree." Betsy spoke quietly, but the determination in her voice was clear. "When someone reveals their true nature, we have to accept it, even if it hurts." She looked at Angus once more, a little sympathy returning in her tone. "I'm so sorry for your loss, Angus, but just as much, I'm sorry that you cared for someone who never existed. That you shared part of your heart with someone who couldn't truly share hers with you."

"But she did," Angus pressed on, guiding the conversation just as he'd sworn he'd be able to do. "You can see a person's soul in the things they create.

There was goodness in her, darkness as well, but goodness too." His voice quavered. "She was going to show me a place that was dear to her. Later this summer she was going to introduce... well..." He gave a sad smile. "To all of you, actually. I was going to fly down and see her home, see where she grew up. Just like my little pool, she was going to share her favorite places with me. There was a little farm she always talked about. With a field of sunflowers and a large oak tree that blazed orange in the fall. We were going to carve our—"

I gasped, then worried that like Pamela, I might have overdone it. Watson reared up beside me, looking startled. "Angus... what did you say?"

He looked over at me as if confused.

I stood, lifting the sketchbook with me. "A field of sunflowers and an oak tree?" I began walking across the space, toward the group, Watson trailing along behind.

Angus nodded. "Yes. She talked about it often."

"Like this?" I laid the open sketchbook on the table in the center of the knitting circle and pushed it toward Angus, coming to a stop directly within the knitters' view.

Betsy gasped as well, but the intake of breath held pain.

On cue, Pamela, Wanda, and Cordelia all leaned in to study the drawing, as if for the first time. Cordelia slowly looked up toward her friend. "Betsy... isn't that...?"

Betsy's hand trembled as she stretched out to touch the sketch of the tractor in the sunflower field. "I can't believe it." Fury laced her whisper. "She drew it?"

"That is James's field, right?" Cordelia pushed on. "I'd know that tree anywhere."

Betsy didn't appear to hear Cordelia, didn't seem to remember that anyone else was even around her. She grabbed the book, glaring at the page as tears began to flow down her cheeks. "She drew James's field? His *tractor*?" Despite the tears, there wasn't sorrow in her voice, nothing but shock, rage, and hatred. "*She drew his tractor!*"

At her yell, Watson wedged himself in front of my legs, growling.

Betsy didn't notice. "She drew his tractor, the very thing she killed him with." With a savage jerk, she ripped out the page, shoved the sketchbook from her lap and stood shakily to her feet, one of her knees popping. She stormed toward the fireplace, carrying the page she'd torn to pieces as she walked and then began throwing them into the flames. "That evil demon. Like what she did wasn't bad enough. She had to gloat about it." More scraps went into the fire. "She probably looked back on this over and over again and laughed, remembered driving over..." She'd thrown the last bits in the fire and whirled back around, having to grip the mantle to keep from falling. "She deserved what she got. I wish I would've known she'd drawn this, that she reveled in it. Not that I'm surprised. She laughed when I confronted her. *She laughed.* It should've been worse, taken more time. I should have...." Her words fell away, and her eyes widened slightly as she realized what she was saying.

"What?" Susan had already been walking toward her. She held out a letter opener with an old-fashioned key at the end, another one of the set that had been used to kill Luca and Alexandria. "Used this in a different way? Not just a quick thrust to her heart? Made her suffer longer?"

Betsy stared at the letter opener, the tarnished metal of the antique key glistening in the firelight. With her lips drawn back over her teeth, Betsy glared up at Susan defiantly. "Yes. I should've stabbed her over and over and over. Do you know what she put James through? How he must've suffered? And then she laughed." She looked back at the blade. "I wish I could do it again."

Susan lowered the letter opener, and with her other hand reach for the handcuffs she'd secured behind her back. "Betsy Whitaker, you're under arrest for the murder of Alexandria Bell."

Betsy was secured in the key room, a rotating shift of
guards assigned by Susan posted at either entrance.
With the phones working, she'd been able to call the
station, but as there was no pending emergency, they
hadn't been able to even give an estimate of when
help would be on its way.

Leo, Watson, and I were on the couch by the fire
in the lobby, Angus sitting across from us.

"Alexandria killed him with the tractor?" Leo
had heard the story, been in on the plan from the
beginning—though he hadn't taken part in the knit
ting circle—yet hadn't seemed able to shake that one
detail. "Seems exceptionally cruel, and rather ineffi-
cient for an official killing."

That particular detail had been new. When she'd
confessed, Betsy didn't hold back, feeling justified in
what she'd done. Her nephew, James, had confided

in her a few months before he died that he'd been involved with an organization called the Irons family. He told her that he'd left it, and that if anything happened to him, anything that looked like an accident, or if he went missing, the Irons family was responsible.

James's death had been ruled a freak accident, just a mishap on the family farm. Betsy admitted she'd believed differently, but she wasn't willing to let her nephew's name, or the family, be tarnished by his involvement in crime.

Angus blinked, and then spoke soberly. "From all we've learned about the Irons family since the truth of Sergeant Wexler came out, it only makes sense that they'd kill him. It's not a group you walk away from. And if Alexandria was a part of it, though it's hard for me to accept, *if* I look at it openly and honestly from the hindsight perspective, *if* I picture Alexandria taking part in such things, it makes a horrible sort of sense that she would do so in a cold yet personal way." His gaze flicked to me. "I imagine you experienced such thoughts as you've looked back on conversations and moments you shared with Branson."

I nodded. "Yes, I have. I know what you mean— though too horrible to even really consider, once you hear the truth, it's hard to fathom how you didn't see it the whole time. Certain aspects of their personalities seemed quirky, or a little difference could be twisted into something dark." I replayed part of my final conversation with Branson. With the warmth of the flames flickering over the left side of my face, I couldn't help but remember that conversation had also been in front of a fire. "You're also right about the Irons family not being something you can walk away from. Branson made it very clear that by making the choice he did, saving me..." I reached across Watson and took Leo's hand. "Saving *us*, he put a price on his head. The same was probably true for Betsy's nephew."

Leo squeezed my hand in response. Instead of letting go, we let our hands rest on top of Watson's flank.

Watson sighed happily and stretched from his place between Leo's and my thighs, mindless of the concerns of those around him, simply content to be warm, well fed, and touching two of those he loved the most.

"But Betsy's claiming she had nothing to do with Luca's death."

Angus gave Leo a puzzled expression. "Of course she didn't. Betsy says she put two and two together easily enough when she heard that Alexandria was part of the Irons family. Betsy was simply enacting revenge... or justice, if you look at it from her perspective. I don't believe Betsy is a serial killer or anything."

"No. I don't either." Leo glanced at me, though I knew he wasn't convinced of my suspicions, I was certain he was fishing for me. "But it still doesn't explain who the other person was with Alexandria that night in Luca's recording."

"No. It doesn't." Angus smiled at me affectionately. "But... I'm betting that will come out in time. And if there's another member of the Irons family among us, I'm certain our resident sleuth will uncover them."

Guilt bit at me for having suspected Angus of killing Alexandria. Even as it did, I couldn't stop from wondering if he'd been the figure beside her in the dark blizzard. He couldn't be. There wasn't a shadow of deception in Angus's eyes or in his voice. And the affection and fondness he'd always shown for me felt genuine, not the least bit forced. To cover both my doubts and my guilt, I made light of it. "Not sure I've earned that trust, Angus. I haven't outsmarted the Irons family yet. I didn't figure out about Branson until it was right in front of my face, and it turns out, the Irons family didn't have anything to do with Alexandria's murder after all."

"Trust me, Fred. If there's anything to figure out, you'll do it." He waved me off, the smile genuine. "And even if there's not, Estes Park is a better place with you in it, safer, and a whole lot more interesting."

Three days later, Katie, Leo, and I stood in front of the newly installed elevator tucked behind the sweeping staircase of the Cozy Corgi.

"You do it, Fred." Katie nudged my arm, urging me forward, excitement in her voice.

"Yeah. It should be you." Leo chimed in his encouragement.

Feeling self-conscious, I stepped forward and hit a little round button. It glowed yellow behind the decorative brass swirls. After a second, the two wood-paneled doors that stood where our old storage closet had been slid apart. Watson growled at the movement and shuffled backward several steps.

Katie oohed. "It's beautiful."

I'd never thought about an elevator being beautiful before, but it was. The small square cubicle was done in glowing wood and aged brass. "It blends with the bookshop and bakery perfectly, doesn't it?"

The doors started to slide shut, causing Watson to increase his growl and back up farther. Leo jumped forward, shoving his hand through the gap in the doors, and caused them to open once more. He stepped inside, then waved us in. "Come on. Let's ride it."

We'd spent two more days at Baldpate, until the roads had been plowed and it was deemed safe enough to leave. During that time, life had returned to normal in Estes, and the elevator had been finished. The bakery was now accessible to anyone, no matter their capabilities. It shouldn't have taken us a year to make that happen.

Katie hopped in and I followed her. When I turned around, Watson was clearly in the middle of a crisis, looking at Leo, to me, then back to Leo. He came forward a few steps, then growling, backed up once more.

Still holding the door open, Leo knelt and held out his hand. "Come on, buddy. It's safe."

I urged him on as well.

Once more, he came a few steps closer, growled, and stood where he was on short, trembling legs.

"I'll walk up the stairs with him." I stepped out.

"It hadn't occurred to me, but I don't think Watson's ever seen an elevator."

Leo pulled me back in and stepped out, taking my place. "No. This is yours and Katie's moment. Enjoy it. Watson and I will meet you upstairs."

Watson pranced around Leo as if in a joyful reunion, but then paused, looking at me in concern as the doors slid closed.

Katie giggled. "I bet you Watson will love the elevator in no time. Something else to be grumpy about."

"You're probably right." Suddenly I realized we were just standing there. "I suppose I should hit the button."

"I think that's how these newfangled things work," Katie jibed. "You'll want to choose the button with a number *two* on it."

"Smart aleck." I grinned at her and hit the button.

The ride was smooth, and it took nearly less time to go up the one story than to take a breath. It was so quick that Leo and Watson were still walking up the stairs when there was a chime and the doors slid open. Katie and I stepped out.

"It is beautiful, but considering how expensive

that thing was, the trip should have been a little longer."

"No kidding." Katie looked over her shoulder as if annoyed, then shrugged. "Well, I guess it just gets people to pastries faster, and that's never a bad thing." She turned and surveyed the bakery's kitchen. "It's going to be strange having people walk through the center of everything. We'll have to make an aisle somehow."

Watson and Leo joined us. "How was it?"

"Speedy." I grinned at him before kneeling to rub Watson's sides. "See? Everyone made it, safe as cucumbers."

At that moment, the door slid shut behind me. Watson flattened his ears, growled again, then trotted off to safety under his favorite table in the bakery.

"There you go." Katie nudged my arm once more. "Told you he'd enjoy being grumpy about it."

At that moment, a knock sounded from downstairs. Watson popped right back up, began to bark, ran across the bakery, passed us, and tore down the steps, as if thrilled for an excuse to get away from the new terrifying contraption.

As one, all three of us exchanged glances, considered the elevator, and walked down the steps.

When I unlocked the door, Cordelia and the other four remaining members of the knitting club bumbled inside. "We saw your lights on, so we thought we'd drop in." Watson approached, and she bent down, obligingly stroking his head.

"Angus was showing us the shop." Wanda motioned over her shoulder. "It was just as beautiful as..." She faltered, then let out a huff of breath as if she was diving in. "Just as beautiful as Alexandria had described."

"I don't know. It's a little too fancy for my liking. Knitting is supposed to be practical, good hard work, and purifying of soul." Minnie scrunched up her nose. "I'm surprised. I'd expect such things from millennials." She made a sweeping gesture toward Cassidy. "But not a man of Angus's age giving in to such frivolity."

Cassidy simply offered a long-suffering expression and gave the old woman a clearly unwelcomed squeeze over her shoulders.

"We're going to be leaving town soon." As Pamela spoke, her gaze traveled over the bookshop and settled on the stairs. "I couldn't leave without seeing the bakery." Her eyes widened, and she looked at me in apology. "And the bookshop too, of course."

"Well, come on," Katie piped up before I could respond, clearly excited to show off the place she loved the most. "I just hate that I don't have the cases filled with things for you to sample. But surely you've got a little time, don't you? I can do a quick lemon bar recipe—it's delicious—at least to be able to have something."

"Really?" Pamela beamed. "Typically, I'd insist you wouldn't go to such trouble, but..." She turned a longing gaze toward her sister.

Cordelia laughed and used one hand to push off her thigh as she straightened from petting Watson. "Wanda and I heard little else besides the anticipation of Katie's baking on the drive out here. I'd say we definitely can make time for that."

Minnie's scowl deepened more than I'd seen over the past several days as she glared at the stairs. "You've got to be kidding me. My knees are aching because of the godforsaken blizzard and snow, and now we have to *hike*?"

Katie practically trilled, and she clapped her hands. "No! Remember, we just had an elevator installed. You'll be our first patrons to try it."

"I hate elevators." Minnie grumbled as she walked by us, earning another squeeze from Cassidy.

Minnie shooed her away. "Good grief, girl, let a woman breathe."

Leo and I watched them go. Watson started to follow, realized we weren't, and trotted back to us. Leo chuckled softly. "They're quite the little group, aren't they?"

"They are. I like them." I could still hear Minnie griping as the elevator chimed its arrival. "They're two members smaller than when they arrived. I hope they'll be okay."

"They seem like it. I have no doubt." Leo turned to me. "Susan called this afternoon. She told me she'd already called you."

I nodded, suddenly tired. I crossed the few steps to the main counter and leaned against it. "She did. What do you make of it?"

Leo and Watson joined me. "I'm more curious what *you* make of it. Are you still suspicious of Angus?"

"I don't know." I considered. "No. I guess I'm not. I say I don't believe in coincidence, at least not very much. And a vacation house being broken into less than a quarter of a mile away from Baldpate during the same blizzard would seem like a pretty large coincidence. Chances are it's Alexandria's mystery figure from that night. Susan thinks so. But still..." I shrugged. "It would be nice to be a little more certain. If they found something definitive."

Leo grinned. "Like some drugs stuffed into the center of a missing skein of yarn?"

"Actually, yes, that's exactly what I mean." I laughed at his expression and shook my head. "I know... if something like that had been found, I probably would've said it was too obvious and clearly planted there. The fact that it wasn't only indicates that the likelihood of the two events being connected has a higher probability."

His honey-brown eyes leveled on mine, growing serious. "What does your gut say?"

"I don't know." I had asked myself that countless times over the past couple of days as we'd finished Percival and Gary's snowed-in anniversary. Every time I looked Angus's way. "I just don't know."

Watson nudged my shin with his hip, demanding attention, or maybe sensing I needed his grounding presence. Either way, I knelt, started to pet, and received a quick lick on my cheek for the effort.

"Did Susan...?" I looked up at Leo, hesitant and suddenly a little embarrassed. "Was that the only update Susan gave you?"

His brows knitted as he knelt on the other side of

Watson. "I think so. Why? Did she give you more details?"

I could tell he wasn't teasing or playing coy, and I was surprised. Susan and Leo had always gotten along, at least as well as anyone got along with Susan. "She didn't send you a video?"

He shook his head. "There's a video? Of the break-in?"

"No, not hardly." I shook my head, and my heart warmed a little more toward Susan. I wasn't sure if the gesture was another one of her goodwill offerings, or simply something she considered the right thing to do for another woman. "It seems…" My gaze darted away. I caught myself. Why was I embarrassed or shy around Leo, after everything? From the looks he'd given, the times he touched my hand since we came back down, he'd more than proven the page we'd turned was going to stay that way, that it hadn't been some fluke of the blizzard. I refocused on his beautiful eyes, even though my cheeks burned. "It seems Luca *did* catch the two of us that night by the fire."

His brows rose. "Oh really?"

I nodded.

"How much?"

"Nearly all. I still have no idea where he was or how we couldn't see him, but he was near enough that he even got our conversation." I hurried on, ridiculous or not, I was self-conscious. "We don't need to worry about the video. Susan said she deleted it before she turned the phone in to evidence. That way it would stay private."

"Really?" Leo looked genuinely surprised. "That doesn't sound like Susan."

I agreed. Which made it even more meaningful. "I told her she shouldn't have, that if they noticed something had been deleted after Luca's death that it could get her in trouble. She empathetically let me know that she didn't appreciate me questioning her skills with electronics."

Leo laughed. "Now *that* sounds like Susan." This time, Leo's blush grew, and his voice lowered. "Did... you watch it?"

I nodded. I had. Despite knowing that our privacy had been invaded by Luca, I couldn't help but be a touch grateful. I got to relive that conversation with Leo, saw the fear and wonder over my face, heard the tremble and hope in my voice. Saw the same reflected in Leo. Got to view and relive our first kiss.

"May... I watch it?" Leo sounded nervous.

"Of course." I couldn't hold back the butterflies from Leo's expression, then wondered why I would want to. "But first, maybe we should..." I motioned upstairs, and as if on cue, laughter floated down to us from the bakery.

"I suppose so." He grinned and then refocused on Watson, releasing a torrent of hair as he ruffled Watson's fur. "What do you say, little man? Want a snack?"

Watson hopped and gave a pitiful yet excited whimper. His wild, manic eyes rolled from Leo to me.

Laughing I pointed upward again. "Katie, buddy. Katie."

Leo's and my affection was cast off to the wind as Watson's nails scrambled in place over the hardwood floor before he shot off, tearing across the bookshop and up the staircase as if he hadn't eaten in a week.

I took Leo's hand and we followed.

Cornbread recipe provided by:

The Baldpate Inn

1917 2017

Estes Park, Colorado

4900 South Hwy. 7, Estes Park, Co. 80517
(970) 586-6151

Click the links for details on Baldpate Inn. Fred and Watson highly recommend booking a room or stopping by for a scrumptious buffet:

Baldpate Inn

BALDPATE INN'S CORNBREAD RECIPE

Ingredients:

- 1 Cup Butter
- 1 Cup White Sugar
- 4 Eggs
- 2 Cups Creamed Corn
- ½ Cup Monterey Jack Cheese, grated
- ½ Cup Medium Cheddar Cheese, grated
- 1 Cup all-purpose White Flour
- 1 Cup yellow Cornmeal
- 4 teaspoons Baking Powder
- ¼ teaspoon Salt

Directions:

Preheat oven to 350 degrees. Using an electric mixer,

cream butter and sugar, then add eggs one at a time. Gradually, mix in corn and cheeses. Stir in the remaining ingredients. Spread evenly in a greased 9 x 13 inch cake pan. Place in oven, close door and IMMEDIATELY reduce oven temperature to 300 degrees. Bake for 1 hour. Top will still seem moist-looking, not dry as with a cake. Center should be set, not gooey. Serve warm.

Although the Baldpate Inn is at the very high altitude of 9000 ft. this recipe works equally well at lower elevations. Just plan to make extra, because even folks that say they don't like cornbread, seem to love this recipe!! It does keep delicious and moist for hours – if hidden!

AUTHOR NOTE

Dear Reader:

Thank you so much for reading *Killer Keys*. If you enjoyed Fred and Watson's adventure, I would greatly appreciate a review on Amazon and Goodreads. Please drop me a note on Facebook or on my website (MildredAbbott.com) whenever you'd like. I'd love to hear from you. If you're interested in receiving advanced reader copies of upcoming installments, please join Mildred Abbott's Cozy Mystery Club on Facebook.

I also wanted to mention the elephant in the room... or the over-sugared corgi, as it were. Watson's personality is based around one of my own corgis, Alastair. He's the sweetest little guy in the world, and, like Watson, is a bit of a grump. Also, like Watson (and every other corgi to grace the world with their presence), he lives for food. In the Cozy Corgi series, I'm giving Alastair the life of his dreams through Watson. Just like I don't spend my weekends solving murders, neither does he spend his days snacking on scones and unending dog treats. But in the books? Well, we both get to live out our fantasies. If you are a corgi parent, you already know your little angel shouldn't truly have free rein of the pastry case, but you can read them snippets of Watson's life for a pleasant bedtime fantasy.

Be on the lookout for Perilous Pottery, arriving Spring 2019!

Much love, Mildred

PS: I'd also love it if you signed up for my newsletter. That way you'll never miss a new release. You won't hear from me more than once a month, nobody needs that many newsletters!

Newsletter link: Mildred Abbott Newsletter Signup

ACKNOWLEDGMENTS

It is with all gratitude that I thank Lois Smith and Baldpate for allowing me to set a mystery in their historic inn. I have such wonderful memories visiting it as a child and appreciate the food, views, and history even more when I visit now as an adult. It is such a treasured part of Estes Park's story. I'm beyond humbled that Fred and Watson were allowed to solve a murder while feasting on cornbread.

A special thanks to Agatha Frost, who gave her blessing and her wisdom. If you haven't already, you simply MUST read Agatha's Peridale Cafe Cozy Mystery series. They are absolute perfection.

The biggest and most heartfelt gratitude to Katie Pizzolato, for her belief in my writing career and being the inspiration for the character of the same name in this series. Thanks to you, Katie, our beloved baker, has completely stolen both mine and Fred's heart!

Desi, I couldn't imagine an adventure without you by my side. A.J. Corza, you have given me the corgi covers of my dreams. A huge, huge thank you to all the lovely souls who proofread the ARC versions and helped me look somewhat literate (in completely random order): Melissa Brus, Cinnamon, Ron Perry, Rob Andresen-Tenace, Anita Ford, TL Travis, Victoria Smiser, Lucy Campbell, Sue Paulsen, Bernadette Ould, Lisa Jackson, and Kelly Miller. Thank you all, so very, very much!

A further and special thanks to some of my dear readers and friends who support my passion: Andrea Johnson, Fiona Wilson, Katie Pizzolato, Maggie Johnson, Marcia Gleason, Rob Andresen-Tenace, Robert Winter, Jason R., Victoria Smiser, Kristi Browning, and those of you who wanted to remain anonymous. You make a huge, huge difference in my life and in my ability to continue to write. I'm humbled and grateful beyond belief! So much love to you all!